That [illegible] ere scam[illegible] ere climbing up from the track, [illegible] rete edge, coming from the shadow into the light. Coming towards him. It was no dream now. He could smell them and hear them and see them. For an instant Gideon's face appeared before him. A mocking face. The round, wide eyes had narrowed into two slits. Then that image faded and there were only the rats.

They were upon him.

Also by Lewis Mallory

GATE OF FEAR

THE NURSERY

Lewis Mallory

NIGHTMARE

Hamlyn Paperbacks

A Hamlyn Paperback
Published by Arrow Books Limited
17-21 Conway Street, London W1P 6JD

A division of the Hutchinson Publishing Group

London Melbourne Sydney Auckland
Johannesburg and agencies throughout
the world

First published in Great Britain 1984
by Hamlyn Paperbacks

Printed and bound in Great Britain by
Anchor Brendon Limited, Tiptree, Essex

ISBN 0 09 934410 6

1

When Theresa was eight years old the nightmares came. They were sharp and vivid and horrific. She had always slept so soundly before but now she woke at night, screaming, or opened her eyes in the morning with the images of the dreams still bright and terrifying inside her. Always she dreamt of the same things. Fire and water, and in the water sprays of blood that made her flinch and cry out.

Dark curly hair fringed her face. Her father brushed it back from her cheek and kissed her, twice – once on each cheek.

'Goodnight, angel,' he said. Then he lifted her up, high above him. 'You'll like having a little sister, won't you?' he asked.

'It might be a boy,' her mother said.

Her mother was sitting in the armchair, leaning back looking heavy and contented, but there were drawn lines of strain at her eyes as if she was thinking, 'It's going on too long.'

Theresa twisted in her father's arms and he put her down on to the thick soft carpet. He sat in his chair and she knelt beside him, but she was watching her mother. If you watched carefully you could see the material of the dress that was stretched over her stomach move. Sometimes the movement was slow, almost writhing, as if an underwater creature was disturbing the surface. Sometimes it was sharp, a kick.

'Does it hurt when it kicks?' Theresa asked.

Her mother smiled at her. 'It's uncomfortable,' she answered. 'Go to bed now, Theresa.'

The bedroom was dark, just one thin line of light

beneath the door. But Theresa wasn't afraid of the dark. The shadows were not threatening. She drifted into sleep with her eyes closing slowly, the room spinning down, the light, the dark, the door, the wall.

The air was hot, strangely hot. There was a moisture about everything, so thick that she could hardly breathe. There was sweat on her face. She mopped it with the end of a scarf that she did not recognise. Blue stripe on black. Very long and silky. And the hand that was holding the scarf, that too was unfamiliar. Tapered red nails. So red they made her shiver in her sleep.

'I won't do it,' she screamed out. But there was no one there, no one with her. She was standing alone. When she looked down she could see the water. Inside her the fire and beneath her the water. The same water. Night after night. Water, whipped up into a spray by the churning bodies. Animal bodies.

'*No*,' she screamed.

There had been someone standing next to her, someone who had gone. But who the someone was and where he had gone to she did not know.

'Come back,' she shouted, yet in the dream she knew that she did not want the person to return.

She was leaning forward, looking down. Flames were all around her, licking at her face, singeing her hair. Flames that came from inside herself. For a moment the water was tempting. It looked cool. The white line of spray rose up to meet her. There was a moment when she almost jumped . She could hear a voice behind her saying, *Go on*. A coaxing voice.

'Don't make me,' she whimpered. 'I don't want to.' And she drew back. She must not jump. She must resist the temptation. She held on to something, clinging with tight fingers. 'I mustn't let go. I mustn't let go,' she thought. But something was pushing her forward. Nothing was touching her but something was impelling her, something that had wormed its way inside her head and whispered with the sound of her own voice.

Let yourself go, Theresa, it said. *Down into the water. Look at the lovely cool water.*

'The fire,' she screamed. 'The fire!' And somehow the thought of the flames held her back from the water, though she did not know why.

Then the voice in her head was gone. She was left in the steaming dark. 'Help me,' she shouted. 'Don't let me fall!'

Her father was shaking her awake. 'What's the matter, Theresa? Is it the same dream?'

'It's in the water, daddy,' she said. 'There's something in the water. Horrible things. And they want me to go in there. But I mustn't, must I? It's so hot and the water is cool. But I hate it in there. I hate the water.'

'Come on now. Try and forget it.' He stroked her hair and rocked her in his arms and when she fell back into sleep he sat beside her on the bed for a while.

The next evening when it was time for bed Theresa sat on the bottom stair in her nightdress. 'I don't want to go to bed,' she wailed.

Her mother was standing by the kitchen door looking at her. 'Go on up to bed, Theresa,' she said. 'I'll be up in a moment to turn the light off.'

'I don't want to,' Theresa whispered, with tears in her eyes.

'Go to bed!' Her mother's voice was stern.

'Don't shout at her,' her father said. 'She's only frightened, because of the nightmares.'

Theresa walked slowly up the stairs and when she reached the top she sat down again. Below her she could see her parents. They were talking.

'She has them every night,' her father said. 'She wakes up screaming. It's been going on for over a week now and I'm worried about her.'

'I'm sorry I shouted,' her mother said. 'I know I

shouldn't. I didn't mean to. You know how it is at the moment, waiting for the baby to arrive. I feel so tense.'

When she looked down between the bars of the banister Theresa could see them clearly. Her father had his arms around her mother.

'Do you think we ought to speak to the doctor about it?' her father asked anxiously.

'I don't think so. It's because of the baby, I expect. We're always talking about it.' She gave a little laugh. 'We talk about almost nothing else. It's become the centre of everything. Theresa's been an only child for the last eight years. It's only natural she feels a bit jealous. But that's all it is. She knows we both love her. I'm sure she'll get over it.'

'But the dreams are so intense.' Her father shook his head. 'When I go in to see her she's covered in sweat, she's really frightened.'

'It's only a bad dream,' her mother said. 'Children often have them.'

'Mmm, I suppose so.'

Her mother turned towards the stairs and Theresa ran into her bedroom. 'I won't be frightened,' she whispered to herself. 'I won't.' She listened to the story her mother read to her and forgot the horrors of the night.

At last her mother said, 'Time for sleep now.' She turned off the light.

In the frame of the doorway Theresa could see her mother's outline. Her stomach was big and swollen. The baby was due, it was almost time. The door closed and Theresa stared at the rectangular shadow and saw her mother's silhouette as if it was still there. She shivered.

And the nightmares came again. That night and the nights that followed.

Her hands were gripping tight on a metal rail. A mist of steam, a small voice behind her. 'Jump,' it said. 'Jump.' A sinister and insistent voice. 'Jump to get away from the fire.'

The water was placid. A flat grey surface, muddy at the edges and bordered by reeds. A large still pond. It was unnaturally quiet, as though waiting for something to happen. She was waiting too. She held her breath. Perhaps they would not come. Perhaps they had gone away and would never return. She lay in the bed for a long time, her eyes behind the closed lids straining to see the thick grey water, scanning the heavy surface for the merest movement. Her heart pounded inside her. Suddenly she let out a wild scream. Two long black shapes were moving steadily through the water. Gnarled and twisted like the bark of ancient trees. But they were not trees. They streamed out from the bordering clumps of reeds into the centre of the vast open stretches of water. 'The crocodiles,' she whimpered.

She was on her knees crying and screaming. 'Remember the fire,' she shouted. 'Remember how it burns!'

Her mother and father twisted and screamed too. She could see their open mouths, turning black. Behind her she could feel . . . When she turned to look there was no one there.

'You will see . . .' Nothing.

No flames, no fire. Just the muddy water and the grey flat rocks. Just the sprays of dank vegetation leaning forward over the water. The flat black surface.

Her father reached out a hand and then was gone.

Theresa closed her eyes but she could still see the water, beckoning her forward. Then she remembered the flames. A column of red topped with smoke. A twisting black cloud that threaded its way into the sky. The orange streaks, sparks dancing brightly over ash and ruin.

'Jump, Theresa, jump! It's what you want.'

'*No*,' she screamed.

Flames of bright evil, fire of sharp death. Driving the voice from her head. When she turned round, no one there. But something was falling. Down over the rail and into the water. A spray of blood was scattered like red glistening jewels over the dark rim of rocks. The writhing scaly bodies, the threshing tails and the points of serried white teeth. The teeth were stripping and tearing, ripping into . . .

Theresa leaned forward to see more clearly, but the coils of steam and the arcs of spray formed a veil. In her hand the metal rail was cold and she leant her head forward to touch it, to feel that cool relief, but there was none. There were the flames and the blood and the surge of movement in the water. 'No,' she was screaming. 'No, no! *No*.'

The same dream. Night after painful night. Then, in screams and blood and agony, her brother was born, and the nightmare left her as though it was rushed away in the waters of the child's birth. The coming of Gideon and the passing of the dream.

In time the impact of the nightmares faded and it was only later, when she was very much older, that she remembered them.

2

'It's Gideon's birthday tomorrow,' Theresa said.

'I haven't forgotten,' Phil told her as he came in through the door. 'Look, I've got him something.' He held up a wrapped parcel. 'I remember when I was twelve, I hope he likes it.'

Theresa looked at Phil with appreciation. 'How thoughtful of you,' she said, going across and kissing him. 'I'm sure he will. He's not very responsive but I'm sure he feels things very deeply. He'll be pleased, I know he will. And perhaps . . .'

She didn't finish what she was going to say but both of them knew that she was thinking, 'Perhaps he will like you better now, perhaps he will learn to trust you.' For Gideon was a strange boy, isolated, very often silent. He had few friends at his school, perhaps none, and only the other day Theresa had said to her mother, 'That's unnatural for a boy of twelve. He should be out of the house more instead of keeping to his room and going down to that cellar. He hardly ever goes out.'

Phil was understanding. He himself had been a bit introverted at that age. 'Don't worry about him,' he always said to Theresa. 'He'll find his own way. He'll be all right.'

Phil kissed her in return. 'I want him to like me,' he said.

She smiled. Phil was a darling. He was twenty-three, three years older than she was and her first really serious boyfriend. 'What have you got him?' she asked.

'It's a secret,' he told her, and put the parcel down on the chair. 'You'll see tomorrow.'

They stood together by the window, looking out across the shady lawn. Trees fringed the green square of grass, giving a secluded atmosphere. Beyond the trees, and out of sight now that they were heavy with foliage, was an ornamental pond in a compact rockery.

'Look, there *is* Gideon,' Phil said, and he opened the window to call out to the boy. Something prevented him, however – a sensation that to disturb him would be an intrusion. He looked so private, so cut off from all around him.

They both stared at him through the open window. He was standing just to the right of them at the edge of the lawn.

‘Can he see us?’ Phil asked.

‘I shouldn’t think so or he’d wave,’ Theresa told him. But secretly she knew that he would not, and quite suddenly a feeling of dislike for her brother welled up inside her. He could look right through people when he wanted to. It was unnerving. She knew that he didn’t like Phil and she resented it.

‘I wonder why he’s just standing there,’ Phil said. ‘He doesn’t appear to be doing anything, or even looking at anything in particular.’

He was as motionless as the trees.

‘He often does that,’ Theresa told Phil. ‘I don’t know why. I don’t understand him.’

Then, quite naturally, and without really deciding to, they both moved away from the window, feeling somehow that even looking at Gideon was an intrusion.

The next day, Gideon’s mother told Mrs MacKenzie, the housekeeper, that they would make a special supper. The two women baked a cake and put candles on it and spent the afternoon in the kitchen making preparations. Yet somehow there was an air of gloom about everything they did. Gideon was such an odd child, unemotional and moody, so unlike other children. When they had moved to this house three years ago, after that trouble at his school, Mrs Tanner had told herself that perhaps the change would help him, that he might make friends and be happier. But nothing had changed. They had moved to this house, a new house in a new town, but Gideon was just the same. He hardly talked at all. Most of the time he sat staring straight ahead of him, or, if someone else was in the room, he stared at *them*. His eyes were cold and distant. It was unsettling.

‘Shall I make ice-cream, Mrs Tanner?’ Mrs MacKenzie asked. The old housekeeper was past seventy, though she never told anyone exactly what her age was. When the

Tanners moved in she had been living in two rooms over the garage, and they had let her stay on. As she had been housekeeper to the previous owners, she continued to run the house even though she was supposed to be retired. She was always active, always busy, and she seemed to thrive on it. And she ran the house so well that now they couldn't have done without her.

'Yes,' Mrs Tanner answered. 'Gideon likes ice-cream. And I'll make some biscuits.'

The two women exchanged a glance. Nobody really knew what Gideon liked, or if he liked anything at all. Then Mrs MacKenzie turned away, shaking her head. She didn't like Gideon, could not stand to be in the same room as him. She got on well with the rest of the family and had a soft spot for Theresa. But Gideon made her feel uneasy. Once she had said to him, 'Stop staring at me that way, just stop staring.' His lips had formed themselves into a smile and the shape was cruel and taunting. She had moved towards him angrily but something had made her stop and turn away, and she had never forgotten that look of his.

Mrs Tanner beat the mixture in the bowl. Gideon would be home from school soon. There hadn't been any more trouble, not like before. She had never found out exactly what had happened; her husband would not tell her, but Gideon had been involved in something terrible and the school had asked him to leave.

Cakes and ice-cream and biscuits, and a special supper. But she didn't know what Gideon would say, probably he would say nothing at all.

That morning she had told her husband, 'Come home early, will you. Remember it's Gideon's birthday.'

'I can't – I'm busy. I've got a meeting.' He made excuses that sounded hollow and insincere. He didn't want to be there. She put her hand on his shoulder and he relented. 'All right,' he said. 'I'll try.'

When Gideon came home from school he sat in the kitchen eating the ice-cream and the biscuits.

'Do you like them?' she asked, putting a brightness into her voice which she did not feel. She was always anxious, always hoping that he would respond normally. But he never did.

He looked up at her. 'I'm going downstairs,' he said abruptly.

The old house had a huge cellar which was dank and dark, but Gideon had recently taken to going down there. It had one bare light and was filled with piles of old discarded junk from the house. Mrs Tanner had gone down there one day to tell Gideon that dinner was ready, and she had seen him sitting in an old armchair. Although he went there often he had never bothered to tidy the place up at all, and he had been sitting in the chair, with the stuffing coming out of the arms, surrounded by old broken suitcases, scattered remnants of magazines, and a mound of faded curtains. In front of him, on the scarred surface of a table, a tall white candle was burning. His arms were crossed on his chest, and his back was stiff and straight. He had stared unflinchingly at the flame. Not a muscle had moved. Intent and fixed, his eyes were like two points, with the candle flame reflected in each black pupil.

'Don't go down there,' Mrs Tanner said with a shudder. 'Stay and have some more ice-cream.'

'I'm going down to the cellar,' Gideon said, not rudely, but almost as if he had not heard her.

She nodded in acquiescence. 'All right,' she said. 'I'll call you when it's time for supper.' She gave him a little smile. 'Mrs MacKenzie and I have made something special for you. And you can open all your presents then.'

'Mrs MacKenzie doesn't like me,' Gideon said unexpectedly.

'You mustn't say that,' his mother told him sharply.

'I heard her telling Theresa yesterday that I was unnatural.'

'You must have done something to upset her. She's a very kind person. She must have been upset.'

'And I don't like her either,' he continued.

'Gideon,' his mother said, but he had already turned away.

'She mustn't say things about me,' he said as he was going through the door.

'Gideon,' she called out, but the kitchen door had closed behind him, and a moment later she heard the door to the cellar being opened in the hall. A few tears forced themselves into her eyes. 'Why is he like this?' she thought.

At seven thirty Mrs Tanner was just putting the finishing touches to the dining-table when she heard the front door slam.

'I'm home, Jean,' her husband called out.

She went to the doorway and kissed him as he came in. 'You're just in time,' she said. 'Supper's about ready.'

'I'll just have a quick wash and then I'll be down,' he told her.

Mrs Tanner went to the kitchen. The housekeeper was placing the dishes on a tray. 'Everything's ready,' the old woman said. 'If you get Gideon, I'll tell Theresa to come in. She's in the garden with her young man.'

There was no one in the dining-room when Mr Tanner came down, so he sat down at the table and waited for them. On his left two places were set for Theresa and Phil, and on his right was Gideon's place. On either side of the boy's plate were his presents, wrapped in bright paper and tied with ribbons. He could see the writing inside a card attached to one of the parcels: '*To Gideon with lots of love from mum and dad.*' He passed his hand over his forehead. Nothing had worked out as he had thought it would. He remembered the night Gideon was born. So much pain.

'I don't think I've known a more difficult birth,' the doctor had said. 'She should have been in a hospital, really. I was about ready to have her moved. But it's over now. It was quick at least, but God, it was tricky. She'll be tired for a while, but the boy seems healthy enough. He'll be all right.

For the first few weeks Mr Tanner had been so pleased to have a son, so proud and so full of plans. A son. A boy of his own. But even as a baby there had been something unusual about Gideon. And as the child grew, so the pleasure faded. That business at school had finished it. It was disgusting what had happened. A laboratory full of dead animals, puffed and bloated and rotting. Some were drowned in little tubs of water. Blood-smeared fur and stiff broken bones. Nobody knew exactly how he had done it but they knew that he was to blame. The school principal had taken Mr Tanner to see the damage. It was sickening.

'He boasted of it to another boy,' the principal had said.

'But how could he have done it?' Mr Tanner had asked. 'How could he have got in here to do it?'

'We don't know that. The door *is* always locked. He won't tell us, of course, but he doesn't deny it. I'm afraid he'll have to leave.'

The memory of those mutilated animals had stuck firmly in Mr Tanner's mind. He hadn't been able to tell Jean. The sight had been too terrible.

Gideon came into the dining-room and sat down. 'Shall I open my presents now?' he asked.

'Of course not. Wait for the others,' his father said sharply. Then, when Gideon stared at him, he suddenly felt hot, as if the air in the room was too close to breathe, and he got up and opened a window.

Just as Mrs Tanner carried in the tray they all heard the sound of Theresa shouting as she ran through the house. The dining-room door was thrown open. 'The fish in the pond,' she cried. 'They're all dead, all of them.'

'What?' Mr Tanner asked. 'What do you mean?'

'The fish are dead,' Phil repeated. He was just behind Theresa.

From down the hall they heard Mrs MacKenzie cry out in dismay. The fish were hers. She looked after them as if they were her children. She fed them carefully and she loved to stand and watch them, to see the flash of gold as they swam through the water.

Mr and Mrs Tanner ran out of the house, with Phil and Theresa following. When they reached the pond Mrs MacKenzie was already there. On the surface of the water floated the bodies of the fish. Gold and white, but no longer gleaming. Already they were becoming dull, and their glazed eyes were turning milky. There was something obscene about the way they drifted slowly from side to side like flotsam thrown up by the current of the sea.

Mrs MacKenzie was crying. 'What's happened to them?' she kept saying to herself.

As Mr Tanner turned he saw Gideon walking slowly up the path. 'You did this, didn't you,' he shouted. 'You killed the fish.'

Gideon shrugged. 'Yes,' he admitted. 'She was horrible about me.' He was staring at Mrs MacKenzie, but in his eyes there was not hatred, only contempt.

'He ought to be put away,' Mrs MacKenzie said in a low voice.

'What did you do, poison them?' Mr Tanner was shaking with anger.

'No,' Gideon replied. 'Not poison, I . . .'

'I don't want to know,' Mrs Tanner screamed. 'It's horrible. What you've done is, is . . . wicked.' She took

Mrs MacKenzie by the arm and led her away to the house.

'You're a monster,' Mr Tanner said. 'A monster.' Then suddenly his anger left him and he felt tired and old. 'Just go to bed, Gideon,' he said. 'Go to bed.'

'I'm twelve,' Gideon replied. His voice was firm and his eyes were fixed on his father's face. 'I'm twelve years old. I'm not a child any more. You can't tell me when to go to bed.'

Mr Tanner began to shake, his anger rising up once more. 'Go away,' he shouted. 'Get out of my sight. I never want to see you again.'

Gideon looked thoughtfully for a moment at his father's upraised hand. 'You can't hit me,' he said quietly. 'You mustn't.'

Mr Tanner slapped his son's face. Once, and then again. 'Go to your room straight away,' he ordered.

Gideon's eyes were clear. No tears. His lips curled into a smile. Then he turned and walked away. His father watched him go and felt something inside himself shrivel and turn cold.

'Come on, dad,' Theresa said, taking his hand. 'Let's go back inside.'

3

He lay on his back in the darkened bedroom staring up at the ceiling. Black thoughts were inside his head. His father had slapped his face. He hated him for that. His father – what did that mean? He felt nothing but loathing for the man who had stood above him with an upraised hand. 'He hit me,' he said out loud into the darkness of the room. He hated his mother too. He hated them all.

They were weak and feeble, and he was strong, stronger than any of them realised. He'd get his own back. He'd shown that Mrs MacKenzie, hadn't he? The shadows on the ceiling above him twisted themselves into grotesque shapes, and the hours of the night passed. He smiled to himself when he thought of the orange fish floating on the surface of the pond. Everyone was against him. Sometimes they pretended to be kind, but he knew they were his enemies. Even his mother. She was on his father's side.

The clock in the hall struck one. As the last chime faded away the silence in the house was re-established. It was even deeper than before. Everyone was in bed. Gideon closed his eyes, and as he lay there on the bed he could see the faces of those he hated. White faces, weak faces. Eyes without power. They were sleeping now, their heads resting on the pillows. All of them, asleep. He could see their dreams. Disjointed and disordered, their little hopes and fears, their secrets. He closed his eyes tighter and the faces in his mind became more vivid and distinct. He saw the mole on his mother's cheek, just below the lip. He saw his father's brows quiver in his sleep, saw Theresa turn over in her bed. Her lips were moving as she whispered to herself in her sleep. The grey papery skin of Mrs MacKenzie's ancient face folded and crinkled with the motion of her breathing.

'I've always been on my own,' he thought, and there was no self-pity in him. 'I don't need anyone. And I've had enough of them. They are burdens. I can't carry them with me.'

The rage was mounting inside him. Opening his eyes from their sleepless concentration he got out of bed and went over to the window. Above him in the dark sky the full May moon shone down over the garden. Its light turned the leaves on the lush trees ashen grey and he could see the silvered surface of the pond. His lips set in a hard line and the bright light from the moon shone through the glass of the window and framed his stony, silent face. For a long time he stood there, scarcely breathing, his small body like a piece of polished glass, sharp in the white light. Then he turned and walked noiselessly from the room.

As he passed his parents' bedroom he glanced at the door and smiled grimly to himself. They had failed him, he had always known that they would. They had been useful, but they had played their part. His bare feet made no sound on the carpeted landing. He drew his eyes away from their door. For a moment he had nearly trembled and he couldn't allow it. He pinched his hand, making it hurt, as though by doing this he would squeeze away all sentiment. The pain made him press his teeth together. 'He hit me,' he thought. And he made himself think of that, made himself concentrate on the shame and the humiliation he had felt. Yet even then, in the midst of the pain, he saw his mother's face and unwillingly remembered that she had always done her best, that she had tried to love him. But he shook his head, as though freeing himself from an unwelcome embrace. She didn't understand, she was limited, and she had said he was wicked. Yes, her too. She was just as bad. All of them. All of them.

Down the stairs. One step at a time. Soft padded carpet. Pink and grey patterns beneath his feet. Lower and lower, till he reached the bottom. Slowly he turned the handle of the cellar door, but though he was careful, still there was a click as the catch opened. He waited for a moment, closing his eyes to concentrate. No, no one had moved. Their faces were still on the pillows. Their eyes were closed and their breathing was deep. He pushed open the door and went down the bare wooden steps to the dark, dim recesses in the depths of the house. He didn't bother to turn on the light. His eyes could see quite clearly all that was necessary to be seen.

On the scratched table top stood a half-burnt candle,

its base a mass of congealed wax. That very afternoon he had sat and watched as the white tallow melted beneath the heat of the flame and then oozed slowly down the slender column.

He picked up a box of matches from the top of the table and struck one to light the candle. At first the flame guttered in the wick. A tiny swaying pinprick of fire. Then it caught, grew steady, became a firm yellow diamond in the darkness.

Gideon sat down in the old armchair and stared at the flame. It was his flame. He could feel it inside his head. Small and bright and hard. His eyes darkened. The flame was in his thought. 'It's too small,' he said to himself. 'Much too small.' And in his mind the flame grew, flickered and jumped and expanded, until it was swelling out to the far corners of the cellar. 'Bigger,' he thought. 'Even bigger. A flame as high as this room, as big as a house.' He wanted the fire to grow, to lick at the pages of the old magazines, to turn white paper brown, to flare at the stuffing of the chair and consume it. In the cellar there were tables and old cupboards. He wanted them to burn. Curtains and discarded clothing, yellowing bed-linen. All of it must go. 'The flame,' he whispered. 'The flame must become a fire.'

His eyes widened as though he were picturing the rush and crackle of a spreading fire. 'Hotter,' he screamed. He wanted it to burn fiercely, this fire.

Theresa woke with the taste of smoke in her throat. It was thick and bitter and made her cough. She sat up in bed and sniffed at the air. Yes, it was smoke. She could see it coiling under the door.

For a moment she stood by the bed, dazed and bewildered. She was still heavy with sleep and unable to think clearly. She didn't know what to do. Her mind wouldn't focus properly. Then she remembered the others. Her mother and father, and Gideon, and old Mrs MacKenzie.

When she opened the door she was met by a roar of flame and a wall of thick smoke. She stood, stunned and frightened, her hand across her mouth trying to keep out the cloying fumes. She could see the flames on the far side of the landing tearing at the door of her parents' bedroom, ripping at the wood, so that the white paint blistered and melted and then flared up.

As Theresa ran down the hall she could feel the carpet hot beneath her feet, and when she looked down she saw the grey wool turn brown, then rise and curl as it began to smoulder.

She started to scream, calling out to her parents in the far room. There was nothing she could do. She couldn't get through to the door. A mass of flames blocked her off. She felt the skin on her feet and legs burning and she turned and ran. 'They'll get out of the window,' she thought. 'I must get round to the front.'

Her room was next to the stairs and, though the paper on the walls was burning, peeling and falling off in long soft ribbons of flame, she forced herself to go down. One finger of flame caught at a strand of paper and floated down across her head. She beat at it with her hands. 'No,' she screamed. The ends of her hair were singed and felt brittle beneath her touch, but she hardly noticed. Above her there was a muffled explosion as the fire leapt from one wall to another. The carpet on the landing was burning fiercely now, and a great blast of heat and acrid smoke followed her as she opened the front door and ran out of the house.

Mrs MacKenzie was standing at the front porch. There was an outside staircase from the rooms above the garage and she had escaped down it. 'Thank God you are safe,' Mrs MacKenzie said.

Theresa was sobbing. Her face was smeared with the grease from the smoke. 'Mum and dad are trapped,' she whimpered.

They backed away from the heat of the fire. Above them the inferno roared, and there was the sound of cracking and splintering wood.

'They'll get out of the window, won't they?' Theresa said anxiously, but when they looked up the windows were already a sheet of orange flames.

'Come away,' Mrs MacKenzie said.

Theresa's face went white. She tried to break away from Mrs MacKenzie, to run back to the house.

'No,' Mrs MacKenzie said. 'It's no use. You can't go back in there.' And when they looked at the front door, it was engulfed in fire. 'There's no way in,' she said.

In the distance they heard the sound of the fire brigade.

'Listen,' the old lady said. 'They'll be here in a minute.' She patted Theresa's shoulder and tried to comfort her.

Theresa was crying hysterically. 'It was awful,' she screamed. 'I called out to them but they were cut off. I just couldn't get there.'

'You were lucky to get out,' Mrs MacKenzie said. Her steel-grey hair hung down over her shoulders. She was shaking uncontrollably, not from the cold night air but from the shock.

'What are we going to do?' Theresa wailed.

But there was nothing they could do. It was all beyond their control.

'And where's Gideon?' she suddenly asked.

'Don't worry,' Mrs MacKenzie said. 'He's all right. I saw him running out of the house when I was coming down my stairs.'

'He got out,' Theresa said incredulously, and mixed in with her tears was a smile of relief. At least *he* was safe.

Gideon stood in the bushes watching the house. His eyes were like two dark stones, impenetrable, glistening like slate that has been washed with rain.

The house was now wrapped in a vast ball of flames. Wild and unruly, they entwined themselves round the wood and brick. From the roof came the sound of tiles exploding and falling. First a crack and then a sliding, grating rush.

From each of the ground floor windows a red billow of fire spat out the glass, and rose in a wide tongue up the white walls, scorching and scarring.

Gideon's face was lit by the yellow flames. His eyes were empty of any emotion. Like dark wells they looked up to the window of the master bedroom, absorbing all that they saw with quiet satisfaction.

'Higher,' he whispered. 'Higher.'

The bushes around him swayed in the night breeze and the gust of heat from the burning house.

At the upstairs window two people appeared. His father was holding his mother, whose mouth was open in a silent scream. The glass of the window shattered and fell in a cascade of bright shards on to the path below. Gideon reached out his hand. For a moment his mind went black. The flames flickered in his pupils and two tears ran down each of his cheeks. Then his hand, which might have been waving, brushed away the tears and his face set hard again. 'It's their own fault,' he said to himself.

The flames at the window lapped at the two figures. White faces, pale and contorted in pain. His father reached forward, a thin and useless defence against the fire. Gideon heard Theresa's voice screaming out. An insistent repetitive wail.

His mother and father were swept by a fan of fire. Still his father's hand reached out. There was a rush of heat and the boy watched impassively as his parents' skin was seared and racked by the tormenting flame.

Then, like a fading frame of film, the figures fell back, disappearing into the whirl of black and orange, subsiding into twisting smoke. From the window where they had stood, a great wash of bright red fire leapt up to the roof. The whole house was burning. A deadly beacon in the spring night.

Theresa's voice had seeped away, to be replaced by the shrill siren of the fire engine as it turned the last corner.

Gideon closed his eyes for a moment. The flames were imprinted inside his skull. He waited for the after-image to fade. Then, shaking his head clear, he turned away and walked blindly into the night.

4

The road passed between flat wide fields. Sometimes there were long stretches of overhanging trees, so that the flat earth to left and right was not visible. At these points the road had the feeling of a tunnel. It was close and hemmed in and very dark. Then the trees ended and it was almost bright. The tall grasses on the surrounding banks cast strange peaked shadows on the night road. At the far end of the road were the outskirts of Stenley, a small market town with the appearance of an overgrown village. It was nearly four in the morning and there was hardly a sound anywhere.

PC Cooper had just come off duty and was driving home down the long empty road. He was tired, but he did not need to give much concentration to driving. There would be no one about at this hour, there never was. It was just a question of getting from the station in town to his brick-built bungalow a mile or two further down the road. He performed the few necessary actions required of him in a flat, mechanical manner, thinking of the hot bath he would have when he arrived home and wondering whether his wife June would wake up when he got in, as she did occasionally, or whether she would remain asleep, as was usually the case. He was driving along, his mind drifting in this way, when suddenly he noticed a figure ahead of him on the road. He hardly saw it at first, because it was in a dark tree-lined stretch, but then it passed into a bright patch of moonlight and became more definite. He stopped the car and got out. It was a boy, and not one that he recognised from the town.

'What are you doing out here at this hour, son?' he asked as he climbed out of the seat of his car. The boy had stopped walking and was standing facing him.

'My God,' Cooper muttered to himself, 'he's in his pyjamas,' and turning back to the car he reached for the blanket which he kept for emergencies. Then he went over and wrapped it round the boy's shoulders. He noticed then that his hair was ruffled and his feet were bare, as if he'd just got out of bed.

'What's wrong?' he asked the boy, but there was no reply.

At the back of his mind he went methodically over all the details of the boy's appearance and manner, making a mental list as though he was recording in a notebook. The boy was bemused, but not frightened. Definitely not afraid. Pale blue pyjamas with darker blue cuffs. Feet, pink from the night's chill, with one toe grazed a little as though he had stumbled. Staring eyes, possibly dark brown in colour. Hair, uncombed and sticking out from his head. It was fair, a very light blond. A pale face with one or two freckles. The face looked quite white in the glow of the moon and the freckles stood out in dark contrast. Age, about twelve years. Nothing remarkable about him except the fact of his being out on the road in this way, and the staring eyes.

'Are you in trouble?' Cooper asked, but as with his previous questions there was no response.

He led the boy back to the car, tried to talk to him, asked him more questions, but there was something trance-like in the lad's movements and he made no reply.

Turning the car round Cooper drove back to the police station. He was feeling tired. It had been a long night. Night duty always took it out of you. He hardly noticed the blue sky begin to lighten and the sun rise.

At the back of the police station he put the car into the big communal garage and, taking the boy by the hand, he led him up the back steps of the building and along a passageway to the reception desk.

'Who have you got there?' the desk sergeant called out.

'I found him wandering along the road a couple of miles out of town. I reckon he's been sleep-walking. There's something funny about him. He seems half asleep still. He hasn't said a word.'

The desk sergeant shook his head. 'A boy's gone missing from that house that caught fire.' He came out from behind the desk and leant down to look into the boy's face. 'Are you Gideon Tanner?' he asked.

There was not a flicker of response, no answer.

Cooper had heard about the fire in the outlying village on his radio when he had been on duty. Two people dead, he had heard.

'Looks like he's in a state of shock,' the sergeant said. 'If it is the Tanner boy, it's no wonder.' He and Cooper exchanged a glance. It seemed likely that it was the boy. And both his parents had been killed. How much did he know, and how much should they tell him?

'Take him in the back and sit him somewhere comfortable,' the sergeant told Cooper. 'Get him a hot drink and I'll phone the doctor to come and have a look at him. I'll make the necessary enquiries, but see if you can get him to talk.'

Gideon was taken into the small room behind the reception desk. Cooper brought him a cup of tea and then sat down opposite him. He was silent for a moment, hardly knowing how to approach this strange child. 'What happened, son?' he finally asked. 'Can you remember? Bad fire, was it?'

Gideon's eyes narrowed. He stared straight into Cooper's face and the policeman felt as if the room had suddenly gone cold. He had a second's irritation but then he shook his head. The lad's parents were dead. He was sorry for him. 'Your name's Gideon, is it?' He was sure it was the same boy. 'Well, you've been through a lot tonight, haven't you.' He smiled encouragingly. 'But you'll be all right, won't you, lad. You're a tough one, I can see. The doctor will check you over. Were you hurt in the fire at all?'

He pulled a blanket round Gideon's shoulders and held the mug of sweet tea to his lips, but the boy made no effort to drink. 'It'll do you good,' he said. Then he sighed. He'd seen some things in his time, but a lad like this, losing his parents . . . It was heartbreaking. 'Where's your gran and grandad live? Are they from round here?' But he got nothing out of the boy. 'Any brothers and sisters?' No answer. And eventually his sympathy hardened. At first he had thought the lad looked lost, shocked, but there was something about the way his eyes followed him that was uncanny and unnatural. Cooper fought down his growing sense of impatience. This was only a boy, hardly bigger than his own son, who was nine years old. No sense in being hard on him. He stood up and paced up and down the room. If only the lad would talk. His silence was heavy and it unnerved Cooper. It set his teeth on edge. The boy's face was turning this way and that, following Cooper's movements.

Gideon watched him carefully, his eyes never for a moment flickering. The pupils were dilated, black and ominous in the brown iris.

'Why don't you tell me what happened?' Cooper

stopped in front of the boy's chair. His voice was a bit brusque, then he modified it. It was important to get the boy to talk now. It would be better for him. His rough-and-ready psychology told him that it would be bad for the boy to bottle it all up. Whatever it was that he had seen it would be best if it were brought out into the open. 'Come on,' Cooper said, not roughly but insistently. 'Now tell me exactly what happened, what you saw. Take your time.' He paused. 'But I want the truth, mind, and it's no use pretending that you've lost your tongue. Now, what happened?' He knelt on the floor and put one of his hands on Gideon's shoulder. 'Come on, lad,' he said encouragingly. His face was on a level with Gideon's. Their eyes met.

'Leave me alone.' Gideon's voice was hard and surprisingly self-contained.

Cooper had been expecting a story to tumble out in snatches, in a trembling and shaken voice, with a tear or two. He was prepared for all that, prepared to be gentle and kind. He knew how to handle children. He had three of his own. But the response that he did get made him rock back on his heels. 'What did you say?' he asked, more disbelieving than angry, but Gideon said no more. His face was set in the same uncommunicative lines as previously and it was hard for Cooper to imagine that he had ever spoken at all. Yet he *had* heard those words. The boy *had* spoken.

Cooper walked to the other side of the room, only a pace or two, then he turned round and faced those eyes again. They were still fixed upon him. Something was going on that he didn't understand. 'If you've got anything to hide,' he began, 'you might as well tell me now. We'll only find out in the end.' Was that a sneer he saw flicker across the boy's face? 'He's treating me like a fool,' Cooper thought angrily. 'There was a fire, wasn't there,' he said. His voice was clipped, precise, as if he was on duty again and confronting a potential criminal. 'How did it start? Do you know?' Cooper sensed that this boy knew something, that he wasn't shocked or tired, that he was in control. The constable passed his hand over his face. No, of course not. He was letting his imagination run away with him. He almost said, 'I'm sorry.' After all, it was only a child he was dealing with.

They stared at each other across the small room. Cooper didn't know what to make of the boy.

The sergeant put his head round the door. 'Any luck?' he asked. 'Has he told you anything?'

Cooper hesitated and the sergeant continued, 'I've got a description. It *is* him. Gideon Tanner. The doctor will be here in a minute or two.'

'No,' Cooper finally answered. 'He hasn't told me anything yet.'

The sergeant shook his head. 'Terrible business,' he muttered, and went out.

Cooper turned back to Gideon, and though his intentions were kindly he again had the feeling that the boy was hiding something. He couldn't explain why, because children who are hiding things are usually more frightened. Yet when he looked at Gideon he had the strangest intuition that the boy had done something wrong. 'Your house caught fire,' he said, but it was as if he was talking to himself, thinking out loud. 'Your mum and dad, killed.' Beyond the door he heard the sound of the doctor and the sergeant talking, their footsteps approaching. Gideon's eyes were staring intently at him. 'You . . .' Cooper began. But somehow he couldn't finish, couldn't complete the sentence, couldn't even finish the thought. 'You . . .' he began again, but a black sheet had folded itself deep down across his mind.

The door opened. 'All right, Cooper,' the sergeant said. 'The doctor's here now. He'll handle things. You might as well get on home and get some sleep. You can make up your report tomorrow.'

Constable Cooper walked out through the door, past the sergeant and the doctor and down the long passageway to the exit at the back of the station.

'He must be tired,' the sergeant said. 'He didn't even say goodbye.'

5

Cooper came out of the door and stood at the top of the steps that led down to the yard. In the distance the church clock in the town began to strike six, but he did not hear it. The sun was fully up now. It slanted across the roofs and threw sharp shadows across the grey stones of the paved yard. Mechanically he walked down. His car was parked in the garage. No sunlight penetrated the narrow opening and he could see that it was dark inside. He blinked his eyes slowly as if he was struggling to come awake, but there was a dull lethargy in his arms and legs and they felt heavy.

'You . . .' The word was thick on his tongue and he swallowed it back. For a moment he paused at the entrance to the garage. A look of surprise flitted across his face and then was gone.

'Must get the car,' he thought. His hand went into his pocket to get out the keys. He shook his head. It was throbbing and aching slightly. There was something he must tell the sergeant. He fought for a minute against the black cloud that washed across him, trying to clarify the thoughts in his mind. He had found a boy wandering along the road. Early morning. A lad in pyjamas. Eyes that stared. Something about a fire. But these things were not clear to him. They were hazy. He hardly remembered anything.

'I must tell . . .' He lifted a hand as if to brush aside the obscuring mists that fogged his mind, but then let it fall back to his side. He did not notice the cold touch of the metal keys in his hand.

'The boy . . . Gideon . . .'

His head was spinning. A darkness was stirring deep inside him. A strand from the trough of his unconscious mind. A curl of something beyond thought, but rising up slowly. A shred of fear.

The boy's eyes were staring at him. Black and brown, then nothing but the black circles. In the ebony facets there was a flicker of movement and then stillness.

Cooper took a step forward. His head felt as if it was splitting in two. He had never had a headache like that before. 'Home,' he muttered. 'I must go home.' June would be waiting for him. She would be up by now, worrying because he was late. Distantly he thought to himself, 'I should have phoned her.' But he couldn't hang on to the image of his wife and his home and his children. The pain in his head and the pressure of those dark eyes drove everything away.

He walked forward into the darkness of the garage. He had left his car in the far corner. He remembered vaguely getting out of the car, taking the boy's hand and leading him into the station, but though he struggled to remember more, after that there was a blank.

'I must go home.' His voice was a feeble whisper. He tried to concentrate but his mind was being torn into shreds. When he pressed his hands to his eyes to squeeze away the pain he could see, like vivid traces on his retina, a criss-cross pattern of bright white lines. A vast and delicate web was forming itself and he could not escape the sight of it. And through the finely strung net something was coming up, breaking the surface.

He opened his eyes. There was his car. Just a few steps

now. Then he jerked backwards. Hanging by a single thread, above the car, was a tiny black spider. Cooper shuddered. He knew it was stupid, but he hated spiders. He had always felt this aversion, ever since he was a small boy. They were ugly little things. He shivered and felt the hairs on the back of his neck rise up in reaction. He had tried to overcome this pathetic fear. It made him feel such a fool. Here he was, six foot tall and a policeman, and he was frightened of spiders. He remembered that time, when was it, six or seven years ago? He had forced himself then. He and June had been sitting in the armchairs on either side of the fire and suddenly she had shouted out, pointing towards the window. There, moving slowly down the curtain, was an enormous spider.

Cooper had laughed. 'There's nothing to be frightened of,' he had said, and making himself go across the room, suppressing his own fear, he had scooped the suddenly scuttling thing into his hand.

'I'll throw it out of the door,' he had said. He hated the thought of killing it, of coming into contact with the moisture of that soft body. The idea of squashing it had made his hand tremble. Those brittle stick-like legs.

'Throw it on the fire,' she had screamed.

'No,' he had told her. 'I'll throw it out.'

He had felt the creature squirming against his palm, and on his skin was the unpleasant tickling sensation of its moving legs. Then suddenly it had bitten him. It had been a horrible shock. He had never thought of spiders biting, never even considered it. He had felt its mouth pinching into his skin, and with a shriek he had thrown it at once into the fire. He had had to watch as the heat shrivelled its legs and dried out the pulpy body.

Afterwards they had both laughed at the incident.

'You're as scared as I am,' June had said.

And it was true.

But this was only a tiny spider, just one small spider.

'There's nothing to be afraid of,' he told himself.

Then his eyes blinked. There wasn't just one of them, there were two, three, no four. He looked again, hardly daring to move. There were dozens of them. Hanging from the rafters, hanging from the roof. The threads glistened in the light from the door. And at the end of each thread swung a tiny spider. There were so many that he could not begin to count them. Some were moving down towards the car. One or two touched lightly against its hard metal surface.

He knew that he would never be able to get into his car, never be able to force himself to push past those wispy threads.

Turning away with a feeling of repulsion he went towards the opening. But as he took a step forward he saw that a huge rope-like web was strung out in the gap. Black strands looped across, joined by intersecting lines. And on the web there were spiders, hundreds of them, crawling like delicate tightrope walkers, with an insidious, careful tread. In the centre of the web squatted a gigantic black spider. Cooper could see the hairs on its body, and its long spindly legs jointed like pointed and bony elbows. The front pair of legs lifted up in a menacing gesture, high and rampant; they seemed to be beckoning to him. It was as if the spider was waiting for him to become entrapped in the fibres.

'It's impossible,' he whimpered. It was a dream, he was sleeping. Soon he would wake up. But it was not a dream. He really was standing there in the garage, trapped and with no escape.

He spun round. They were everywhere. There were tears of fear and frustration in his eyes. 'Please,' he cried. 'Please, let me out.' A sob of despair. As he stood there he saw that they were coming closer. Small and large, they came towards him. From the roof they were dropping down. Closer, closer, creeping across the car, along the floor.

There were different kinds. Small gingery-red spiders with curled legs and round plump bodies. Some were flecked, black with white. These were mainly round the walls, working their way incessantly from one side of their surrounding webs to the other as though in pursuit of food. Then there were the black ones, elongated bodies with angular legs and eyes that protruded. Sometimes they would be still in corners and then suddenly they would dart forward with frightening rapidity. The light from the door was brighter now and the more it came the more he could see.

'I want to go home.' His voice was like a boy's, a child's, begging, pleading. He felt something brush against his hair. 'No,' he screamed. His body ran cold at the thought of the contact. He slapped with his hands, trying to push it away. But there was another. A soft touch on the skin of his cheek.

They were grotesque. Legs lifting in pairs. A brittle step forward. Closer. Eyes bright in the flat faces. On the largest of them he could see the line of the mouth.

'They bite,' he thought. 'They bite!' He had a fleeting memory of that itch on the palm of his hand.

He was slapping at his face, trying to get them off. They were in his hair, twisting it with silken thread. When he looked down, the floor was a seething mass of movement. And all around him they floated on the thin spun strands.

He turned dizzily, desperately trying to be free of them, but he was afraid to move and dreaded feeling the squelch of their bodies under his feet. The sick rose up inside him. He could taste it in his mouth. He tripped and fell back against the car, and with a rush and scuttle of legs the spiders scrambled over him. Like dots of clinging soot they attached themselves to his skin. Only, unlike soot, they were slimy and cold to the touch. He lay on the ground in rigid fear, feeling them move inside his clothes, work their way along his legs, creep beneath his loose-fitting shirt. The large ones crouched low in the confined space. He could feel the scrape of their bodies as they dragged across his skin. The small ones scurried, feather-like in their touch. And all the time more were coming.

Then he could feel their mouths, opening and closing on his flesh. Pinpricks of pain. He rolled over and felt them wriggle and squash beneath him. He sensed, rather than felt, the watery discharge as their bodies burst.

Struggling to his feet he ran blindly, conscious of spiders beneath his tread. They were clinging all over him. Mouths and legs and hairy bodies.

He ran as fast as he could, but they were in his eyes. He could see nothing. With all the force of his heavy body he hit the wall, crashed into it head first. The bones of his skull cracked like eggshell under the force and Cooper sank down in a mess of his own spurted blood to die in the quiet corner of the garage.

6

After the fire Theresa was admitted into hospital, and she was to remain there for the next two weeks. The skin on the lower part of her legs was badly burned and her feet, in particular, were very painful. One side of her face was raw and blistered, though not severely, and she was relieved to learn that it was unlikely there would be any permanent disfigurement.

For the first few days after her arrival her body had been stiff and in great discomfort. The surface of her skin, dry and cracked as old parchment, was sore, and sensitive to even the slightest movement. Gradually, however, as the days passed, she began to recover. Unpleasant as the burning was, it was classed as only superficial. In a few days the swelling around the worst areas had begun to pucker and subside. By the end of the first week she was beginning to feel quite normal in physical terms. She had had to have her hair cut, of course, for the fire had left it coarse as stubble, and the sight of herself in the mirror, with the red-streaked skin and short cropped hair was unfamiliar and gave her a feeling of strangeness. She stared into the mirror in the hospital ward and hardly recognised herself.

Every day as she lay on the white-covered bed Theresa cried tears of anguish at the thought of her parents, reliving in her mind, over and over again, the terrible details of their death. She kept picturing the two of them at the burning window, she was plagued by the memory of her father's thin and ineffectual arm striking out to combat the rising flames. At first, unable to move because of the pain, she cried in a sort of stiff immobility, clenched on the bed, with silent tears gushing from her eyes. But she was hardly aware of the tears. They just flowed from her, almost without her consent. The nurses were constantly dabbing at her face and changing the pillowcases, which quickly became sodden. In the second week she cried less, but more forcefully, throwing her body this way and that on the bed, as though by doing this she would cast out the awful pictures in her mind and drive the dreadful memories away from her. The upheld thin white arm. Its wild beating at the surrounding smoke-filled air. The two pale faces, mouths open in the formation of a silent scream.

By the end of her second week's stay in hospital there were periods in which she was able to think of other things, but even so, when the memories came they were as severe and violent as ever. Perhaps more so. The vivid horror was a dreadful contrast with the white peacefulness of the hospital, and, sometimes, staring at the flat white bed and the pale surface of the walls seemed to induce an even greater awareness of the tragedy. The almost silent atmosphere of the hospital seemed scarcely real to her at times. Beyond the quietness she lived again in a world which was composed of sheets of red flaring flame, swirling smoke, and harsh smells of burning wood. Her ears were filled with the sound of the splintering crack of house timbers. The sharp and frightening noise penetrated the quiet ward where she lay, and she crouched deep in her bed as though fearing that the ceiling above would come crashing down.

Then the day came when she was going to leave the hospital. She sat up in bed, restlessly waiting. To move was sometimes still painful. The skin on her ankles remained red and sore, but the blisters had hardened into scabs and peeled away.

Phil was coming to pick her up today. He'd been marvellous the last week or so, coming to visit her every day, finding somewhere for her to live, looking after Mrs MacKenzie, and checking up on Gideon.

'I can't understand why he's in a mental hospital, there's nothing wrong with him,' she had said one evening. Now that their parents were dead she felt the need to protect her brother. 'He may be strange sometimes but he's not mad.'

'It doesn't mean anything,' Phil had explained. 'Don't worry about it. It's just that he was in a kind of trance – from the shock, they think.' He shook his head. 'He hasn't spoken, hasn't uttered a word. The doctors are worried about him. They want to keep him under observation for a while. They say he should come out of this trance thing in a day or two, especially after he's seen you.'

'We'll go straight away. As soon as I get out of here, on Tuesday afternoon,' Theresa had said emphatically. 'It's the first thing we'll do.'

'No,' Phil had said, shaking his head. 'Don't let's rush things. I've found you a little flat. It's very small, but it will do for a few months, until we can get married. You could stay with me, but you know how crowded it is at home.' He had touched her hand. 'After we're married we'll get something bigger – for the three of us. But for the moment this flat will do for you . . . and Gideon. The first thing we ought to do is get you moved in there, get everything ready so that Gideon can come home to somewhere settled.'

'You're right,' she had said. 'Let's make the flat ready and I'll go and see him on Thursday or Friday, and perhaps he'll be well enough then to come home with me for the weekend.'

But now she didn't want to wait. She wanted to go and see Gideon, and really, she wanted to take him with her straight away. She couldn't bear the thought of him in that place.

The nurse brought her her clothes and drew the curtains round the bed. 'Poor Gideon,' Theresa thought. 'It's bad enough for me, but at least I've got Phil.' She was warm-hearted and generous and, characteristically, she forgot the differences that she had sometimes felt, forgot her recent antagonisms. All she thought of was the boy who had been orphaned, her brother. Just twelve years old and he was all alone, except for her. 'I'll do everything I can for him,' she thought fiercely. 'I'll look after him.' They would set up home in the little flat that Phil had found them and she would try to make up for everything that he had lost.

As she dressed she thought eagerly, 'There can't be anything wrong with him. But he must be so lost and lonely. Poor kid.'

The previous night she had lain down on the bed thinking of the new flat, making plans, wondering what it would be like. But in the half-darkness of the ward an eerie silence had seemed to engulf her and drag her away from the happy thoughts of Phil and the home she would make for Gideon. As she had drifted off into sleep she had seen a veil of flames, the staring eyes of a dead fish, a bright orange sun rising over a flat mirrored sea. Water. Grey, and shiny-surfaced. There had been a voice too, whispering to her insistently, but it had been a long way off, and although she was disturbed she had turned over in the bed and brushed away the irritation of her dream. Only then had she slept soundly.

The nurse put her head round the curtain. 'Your fiancé's downstairs waiting for you,' she said.

'Oh, tell him I won't be a minute. Thank you.' It took her longer to dress than she had expected. Shoes felt unaccustomedly hard and hurt the sides of her feet. She practised walking up and down by the side of the bed until she felt steadier. Her hands shook a little as well, because she was thinking that while she had been lying there time had been passing. The world had been going on, without the existence of her parents. It was two weeks now since they had died. Already they belonged to the past. Her eyes clouded over with tears at the thought of the world without them and she had to sit down on the bed again to try and regain her calm. But at last she was completely dressed and ready to go down to Phil. She wasn't sorry to leave the hospital – although everyone had been kind to her – because of its association with the terrible night of the fire.

Together she and Phil went in to see the doctor.

'Don't do too much,' the doctor said. 'Keep off your feet as much as possible for the first few days. No long walks or any great exertion.' Then he noticed Theresa touching her hair and running her fingers over the scarred skin of her temples. 'Don't worry about that,' he reassured her. 'The hair will grow quite normally, and you were very lucky with the burns. They're not too bad at all. The skin will heal and it will grow back just as good as it was before.' He made an appointment for her to come back as an out-patient. 'Just for a check up,' he told her.

And then, at last, they were outside the hospital. It was a beautiful June morning. The sun was rich and warm, without being too overpowering, and the sky was quite cloudless.

'I'm so happy to be alive,' she suddenly said to Phil, impulsively. 'In spite of everything. In spite of all the suffering.'

He squeezed her hand, knowing how she felt, and the two of them stood together for a moment in the street outside the hospital, taking in the sweet sunshine, seeming to gain strength from it. The lilacs and laburnums in the surrounding gardens made bright patches of colour, and the scent of lavender and stocks drifted across to them.

For the first time since the accident Theresa felt a sense of peace inside her. In that moment, standing with Phil, by the low brick wall of the hospital, the future suddenly seemed possible to her. For two whole weeks she hadn't really known how she would be able to go on, with the dreadful memories so deep inside her. Now, she began to see that she would be able to continue living, and would be able to take a pleasure in things again. She was grateful for all the surrounding colour and the soft fall of the sun across her face, and she was grateful too that Phil was standing close beside her. 'I love you,' she said to him, and he squeezed her hand again.

7

Gideon sat in an armchair in the day-room of Glendale, and he was watching everything. There were only fourteen patients in his wing, none of them seriously ill, and in the daytime they all sat in the day-room or walked about in the gardens, under the eye of the nurses. Sometimes Gideon went out and walked across the lawns as well, but he preferred to sit in here, liked listening to the conversations of the other patients and the passing comments of the nurses. When he had first come here, the others, all older than him, had been keen to talk to him and to welcome him to their little circle. But he hadn't wanted to speak to them and he disliked it when they came across to him. Now, because of his detachment they usually left him alone, only occasionally calling over to him or coming to talk to him. If they spoke to him he ignored them, showed them that he was not interested by turning his head away. But still he liked to watch, and also to listen.

The only patient who made a persistent effort and continued to speak to him whatever he did, was Williams, the man he shared a room with. Williams was in his twenties, with slightly vacant face and empty pale blue eyes. Williams had tried to kill himself. Gideon had heard the nurses talking about it. So he watched Williams with a special interest and fascination. They had brought Williams in here because he had tried to hang himself, and they kept him because he believed that someone else was responsible. On Gideon's first night Williams had whispered to him, 'I'm getting better. Someone tried to kill me but they made a mess of it. They can't kill me. I'll be all right. I'm getting better.

Sometimes Williams got angry with Gideon for staring at him.

'Don't stare at me,' he had said once. 'Perhaps it was you.' Then he had smiled. 'I'm only joking. You're too small. You're only a boy. The ones who did it were big, and horrible, and ugly. You wouldn't do things like that to anybody, would you?'

Now, Gideon sat in the armchair looking out through the window at the patch of lawn where Williams and one or two of the others walked between the rose-bushes and the pine tree. He liked sitting here, watching all the movement outside and being aware of everything that went on in here. He felt at the centre of everything, as if he had them all within his grasp. Williams was his special interest, though. He leant forward a little as Williams disappeared behind the ornamental hedge. A slight frown passed over his face, as if he was annoyed that he could no longer see Williams. But then the thin body turned back the way it had come and passed into sight again. Gideon sank back in the chair and turned his attention to the room.

Two of the men were playing table tennis. They were slow, as though they had not played the game before. When the balls fell to the floor they spent a long time searching for them, as if they had no particular enthusiasm to go back to the game. Yet they played at the table every day. Over in the far corner another man was painting, totally absorbed in the task, hardly ever looking up. Laboriously, he dragged his brush across the paper and then dipped it clumsily into the pot of water. At least three times during the morning he would spill the pot of water and a nurse would rush over and mop up the mess, saying, 'Oh dear, you've done it again.'

Everyone else was watching television. Occasionally there was talking between them, but mostly they were quiet, following the movements on the screen attentively with their eyes. One programme followed another, and whatever it was it held their interest to the same degree. Sometimes a little laugh passed round the group, and when that happened one or two of them would look over to where Gideon was sitting, as though they wanted to include him in the current joke. He avoided their eyes.

It was three o'clock. Time for Dr Richards to walk around the ward. Gideon listened for the sound of his footsteps in the corridor beyond the day-room. At last he heard them.

Nurse Simpson met the doctor at the door, and together they walked around the room, stopping occasionally while Dr Richards chatted to this person or that. Then they were by Gideon's chair. He sat still, not showing the exasperation he felt at their presence. He hated them, he wanted them to leave him alone, but he knew it would be wiser to say nothing.

'And how's Gideon today?' Dr Richards asked.

There was a brief hesitation while the doctor and the nurse waited to see if Gideon would answer for himself. Then Nurse Simpson said, 'He's coming along very nicely.'

The doctor patted Gideon on the head. 'Well, I'm glad to hear it,' he said.

Gideon sat stiffly, irritated by the feel of the hand on his hair. He blinked a little.

'He's got a very good appetite,' Nurse Simpson said with a humouring laugh.

'You're going to have a visitor in a day or two,' Dr Richards said. 'Can you guess who that might be?'

Again the hesitation.

'Well, it's your sister Theresa. That's a nice surprise, isn't it? Are you looking forward to that? I'm sure you are.'

'How old is she?' Dr Richards asked him. 'She's a bit

older than you, isn't she?' Then the doctor decided to take a calculated risk, to try a shock tactic. 'Did you escape with her when your house caught fire? You *did* know she got out all right, didn't you? We told you, didn't we? Do you remember?'

Gideon's eyes were steady and unwavering. He would not let them get to him. He tightened the muscles in his arms.

'It was a terrible fire,' the doctor said. 'Do you remember *that*?'

Gideon turned his head to one side and looked out of the window again. Williams was standing quite still by the hedge, looking up at the branches of the distant pine tree. Suddenly he began to scream. He threw his arms about as if warding off an attacker. At last he flung himself on to the ground, and they could hear the muted sound of his sobbing.

The doctor and the nurse ran out through the French windows and hurried across the lawn to Williams' prostrate body. A smile flickered on Gideon's lips.

At the ward meeting later that afternoon Dr Richards sat behind the desk in his office, with the ward sister and the two duty nurses facing him. The orderlies had been left, with one remaining nurse, to keep an eye on the patients while the meeting was on.

For most of the time Richards and the nurses discussed Williams' case.

'I thought his position had stabilised,' the doctor said. He passed his hand over his forehead in a gesture of impatience. 'We agreed that it was a fairly straightforward case. Four to five months of medication and care, and he should have recovered satisfactorily. Here we are at . . .' He consulted the file notes. '. . . Fifteen weeks and he seems to be relapsing for no good reason.'

'This last week he's become very agitated,' the sister

remarked.

For a long while they went over his case, the background to the phobia, the structure of the neurosis, the social factors.

'Keep him under close supervision,' the doctor said finally and with that they passed on to Gideon.

Dr Richards shook his head. 'It's obviously a deep-seated trauma,' he said. He looked round at the other members of staff. 'I don't think it's really all that serious. Just one isolated area of blockage that is manifesting itself in this repeated refusal to speak.' He paused. 'I take it he hasn't said anything yet?'

'Not as far as we know,' the sister said. 'He still seems to reject the approaches of other patients.'

'Mr Williams,' Nurse Simpson said, 'has mentioned to me that he talks with Gideon.'

'Have you seen Gideon talking to him?' the doctor asked her.

She had to admit that she had not, although she had noticed Williams talking to the boy.

'I think the only worrying thing,' Dr Richards said, 'is that none of us, as yet, have been able to make contact with Gideon. We've all of us tried, but we haven't had any success. His sister was on the phone to me earlier this afternoon. She just came out of hospital herself this morning. You all know the background to Gideon's case. She wanted to come straight round and see him. Natural enough, I suppose. But I persuaded her to wait a day or two. I thought we might be able to use her impending visit as a way of drawing Gideon out. His increasing anticipation might lead him to become more forthcoming. I'd like one of the nurses to spend nearly all her time with Gideon prior to the visit. It is possible that the constant attention might help him to relax somewhat.' He frowned. 'We've got to get him to talk. That's the most important thing.' He sighed. 'It's not going to be easy for the lad. He might have seen his mother and father die in that fire, and that's a big thing for anyone to come to terms with. But still,' he added, by way of finishing off, 'getting him to speak is the main thing at the moment.'

The sister was smiling at the doctor. 'We've already anticipated you a little, Dr Richards,' she said. 'We were talking about this before your afternoon visit. Nurse Simpson has already volunteered to spend tomorrow with Gideon, to see if she can bring about any improvement.'

'Good,' the doctor said. 'We'll give it tomorrow and the day after that. If nothing's happened I'll tell his sister that she can come in on Friday.'

Soon after that the ward meeting came to an end. Nurse Simpson was just about to go off duty. She walked down the corridor past the doors of the day-room. Looking in through the glass panels, she saw Gideon sitting alone in the same chair by the window that he had occupied all afternoon.

8

The sleeping-area in Gideon's wing of the hospital was divided into eight compartments, each with two beds. At the present time two of the beds were vacant. Each cubicle was open-fronted, arranged around a central area where a night nurse sat at a duty desk. Thus, without even moving, she could see into each of them. But at the same time a sense of privacy was created for the patients, who shared their little room with only one other person. There was a window at the end of each cubicle, and in Gideon's, which faced east, the sun was already beginning to glimmer. The nurse on duty looked at her watch. It was just five o'clock.

Gideon was wide awake. He lay in his bed without moving, listening to the rapid breathing coming from the other bed and the occasional mutterings as Williams twisted and turned in his sleep. Williams had slept heavily last night. Gideon knew that they had given him an extra sedative. The pink glowing sun spread its rays across the glass, lighting up Gideon's watching eyes. He was thinking to himself, 'I'll soon be out of here. Theresa will come and take me away.' Then his face darkened. He would not talk to them. There were so many things that were beyond their understanding. He mustn't let them find out anything. Theresa would get him out. He only had to wait for her to come. She was his sister. She would look after him, and do what he wanted. He breathed a sigh of relief at the thought.

Outside the window the birds were beginning to sing. A sharp and strange little chorus. Gideon lay for a long time listening to them.

At seven o'clock the night nurse went round waking people up. Gideon washed and dressed and sat beside his bed. Williams came awake slowly, as if he resented leaving the dreams of sleep. At last, pulling himself out of the bed, he put on his shabby dressing-gown and shambled to the bathroom. His feet in their old leather slippers, made a scraping sound across the wood floor.

When he came back from his wash he was more alert. His sly, mistrustful eyes slid from side to side, constantly moving. He sat on the side of his bed and took out a packet of biscuits from the bedside cabinet.

'Want one?' he asked Gideon. But, as if he knew he would get no answer, he did not proffer the bag. He just took one out and began to chew restlessly.

'I'm getting better,' he whispered. 'I really am. I'm getting better.' He frowned. 'What happened yesterday?' Then he answered his own question. 'I fell over, didn't I?'

He nodded his head, as if the memory was coming back to him. 'Somebody was hurting me. You know what happened, don't you.' He gave Gideon a half-hidden, collusive smile. 'But I'm not going to tell them. You know, and I know, but they don't know. And we won't tell them.' Then suddenly he looked suspicious again. He stopped chewing the biscuit. 'You won't tell on me, will you?'

Gideon averted his eyes, irritated by Williams' rambling.

'Nurse Simpson's going to look after you today,' Williams said. 'They were talking in the bathroom. You're going to have Nurse Simpson all to yourself.' He looked back at the nurse at the desk as if he didn't want to be overheard. Then he said in a lower voice, 'They do that sometimes. They're going to try and get you to talk. But you don't want to, do you? They did that to me. They wanted to get me to give myself away. But I wouldn't. I know what they're up to.'

Gideon frowned. He was perturbed by Williams' words.

'You'll have breakfast with Nurse Simpson in Sister's room. They pretend it's a treat. Then she'll take you for a walk. She might take you to the lake on the other side of the fence. They never took me there.' He sighed as though he still bore the grudge of that. 'And all day long she'll be with you.' His eye had a far-off look. 'She'll stay by your side, talking softly, being kind.' He sneered. 'Oh she'll be kind, all right.' Then suddenly he sat up straight. 'I'm getting better,' he said. 'I fell down yesterday but . . .' He looked at Gideon, their eyes holding together for a moment. Then Williams flinched away with a moan, rolled over on to his side and curled up his body.

Williams was right. At eight thirty Nurse Simpson came to fetch Gideon. The others were going to the day-room for breakfast.

'Come on, Gideon,' she said cheerily. 'We're going to have a special treat. We'll have breakfast all by ourselves in Sister's room.'

Gideon sat opposite Nurse Simpson in the improvised breakfast-room. Some effort had been made to give the room a certain air of informality. A little chequered cloth lay over the usually bare table, and a pot of flowers had been placed at the centre.

Nurse Simpson smiled prettily across the flower tops, trying to engage the boy with her eyes. 'Eat up your cereal,' she told him. 'I've asked the cook to scramble us some eggs.' Scrambled eggs were considered a special breakfast in the hospital. 'You haven't put on any sugar,' she commented. 'Here, let me do it for you.' She got up from her chair and came round to Gideon, sprinkling a liberal amount of brown sugar on to the cornflakes. 'That looks a lot nicer, doesn't it,' she said, looking at the little piles of glistening golden brown. 'We keep brown sugar for treats,' she added, trying to make him aware of all the little privileges she was arranging for him. But she did not apply pressure when he made no response, did not try to force him to speak. She went back to her seat at the other side of the table, saying, 'It's a beautiful morning, isn't it? I think you and I should go for a nice walk together after breakfast.'

'Is there anything special you'd like to do?' she asked, when breakfast was finished. 'No? Then let's have that walk, shall we?'

Outside in the bright sunlight the nurse tried to take Gideon's hand. But he pulled it away; he wasn't going to have that. She didn't mind his reaction, however; in fact, she was almost pleased by it. Sometimes a negative response was the beginning of the breaking down of a block. Perhaps he would get angry, would begin to scream at her. She was prepared for that to happen, knowing that the fury would eventually dissolve into tears and that afterwards Gideon would respond more naturally.

They walked side by side across the lawns, through the metal gate in the fence that was carefully concealed in the hedge, and then along the path that led to the lake.

'Let's sit down.'

There was a bench by the water's edge. Gideon sat down obediently.

'I've been wanting to have a talk with you,' Nurse Simpson said. 'A proper talk. Just the two of us.' She made it sound like her own wish rather than part of a prescribed treatment.

Gideon stared ahead at the still surface of the water. He hardly listened to what the nurse was saying.

After a while, aware that his attention had drifted away from her she put her hand on his arm. 'Gideon,' she said in a coaxing manner, 'did you hear what I said?'

Abruptly, Gideon withdrew his arm from her touch. 'Leave me alone,' he said. 'I don't like you to touch me.'

There was something like a gleam of triumph in the nurse's eyes. She had got him to speak. Because of this she forgave him the hostility in his tone, saying to herself that it was only to be expected. 'Oh, so you haven't lost your tongue. Well, I am glad about that. I was just about to tell you that your sister Theresa's coming. Probably on Friday. What do you think of that, then?' She got up and walked over to the water's edge. She was looking down into the muddy shallows. She felt that at this moment she shouldn't be the first to talk, so she waited for a few seconds to see if Gideon would answer her question. She knew that if he remained silent she could soon pick up the thread of conversation and try again, but if he should happen to speak, it would be so much better. The minutes dragged by, then behind her, amazingly, she heard his voice. His voice was soft and she couldn't quite hear the words.

'Water is wet, glassy as an eye that you can look into. Take me into the water and let me know how it is beyond the reflecting surfaces. Down deep, past the rushes, past the choking weeds. Down in the hidden parts. Let me look there. I'll dive through the surface of things.'

His voice was flat and monotonous. Although Nurse Simpson strained to hear, it was impossible. But she did not move, afraid that if she turned round it would inhibit him.

'Water, still and deep and cold. Beneath it and inside it are . . .' He whimpered softly. 'Theresa,' he called. Then louder, 'Don't touch!' He was laughing softly to himself. There were things he could see – the lake, the nurse, the trees on the far shore – and something beyond the surface of the water that he could not. 'I expect there will be pain,' he said. His voice was cold and hard, admitting no emotion. 'But it cannot be allowed to matter.'

Nurse Simpson turned back towards him, took a step closer. 'Pardon?' she said. 'What did you say?' But Gideon was silent. She tried to get him to talk again, but without result. It was as though there had been just one thing he had needed to say. He remained impervious to all her entreaties.

Later, they walked back to the hospital for lunch, and then in the afternoon they went into the gardens. She found a secluded place for them in the rose arbour. Gideon did exactly as he was told. 'Let's walk here.' 'Let's sit here.' 'Look at those flowers.' But, whatever she said, he did not reply again.

Every so often Nurse Simpson said, 'Your sister's coming to see you. You're looking forward to that, aren't you, Gideon.' Or, 'What's Theresa like? It must be nice to have a sister.' Questions to lead him out of his silence.

And as the afternoon dragged on Gideon began to hate Nurse Simpson. Her soft and gentle kindness, her enthusiasm, the invidious and transparent questions. Most of all he hated her lack of understanding. He walked by her side or sat in the rose arbour, his eyes forever fixed on some unseen distant point. But inside his eyes there was a lambent flicker.

Sometimes, when Nurse Simpson looked at him, he made her feel cold. That morning she thought she had made a breakthrough; now she was convinced that she had not. He sat beside her, stiff and stonelike. Did he think of anything at all, sitting there like that, so immobile? She didn't know. And though she talked on, trying to do her job as best she could, and to help this curious and lonely boy, she was relieved that it would soon be time for her to go home. For try as she might, to be nice to Gideon, she could feel a growing sense of dislike for the boy. There was something in his staring eyes that seemed almost cruel.

At five o'clock the sun was slanting across the slate roof-top of Glendale, and the base of the pine tree was already in shadow.

'Well, we'd better get you inside,' Nurse Simpson said. 'And we'll have another day tomorrow just like today, shall we?' She put an enthusiasm into her voice which she did not feel. 'We'll have you talking tomorrow,' she added, almost as a form of self-encouragement.

Gideon turned his head and looked at her. He stared at her full and hard. He wouldn't let her talk to him again, he wouldn't.

She was a little shaken at the look of fierce hatred in his eyes. It quite unnerved her. She could hardly bring herself to smile. Her heart beat quickly inside her and she stood up abruptly to cover up her confusion. 'Come on, Gideon,' she said. 'I'll take you back to the day-room.' And she was thinking. 'There's something awful about him, there's something uncanny.'

9

It wasn't a long walk from Glendale to the flat which Nurse Simpson shared with three other girls. She had to go across the park and then up the long avenue. She always enjoyed the walk, whatever time of year it was, but now, in early summer, it was particularly pleasant. At this time of evening, just before six, the park was almost deserted. It was too late for the home-going children and too early for the evening strollers.

She came out of the hospital and walked down the drive to the main road. In the distance she heard the long drawn out howl of a dog and she frowned at the ugly sound. When she was standing at the kerb it came again. A low wailing sound. It made her shiver, but there was no dog in sight and when the noise ended she forgot about it.

When there was a break in the flow of traffic she ran across the road and went through the wide black gates of the park entrance. She always took the same route. It wasn't the quickest but it was the one she enjoyed most. Up the path to the brow of the low hill. Below, in the distance, the tops of buildings framed the boundary, and she stopped for a minute to look down over the green descent. At this point she always left the path and veered off to the right towards the copse of oak trees. After that there was another path which she joined, which led through a series of undulations to the distant north gate. On either side of the path massive bushes of rhododendrons leant towards each other. She loved the exotic bushes, with their heavy waxen leaves and clusters of crimson or delicate pink flowers.

She walked along the path between the bushes, sometimes stretching out her hand to touch an overhanging leaf. The smell in the air was heady and rich, almost overpowering. She had no special plans for that evening. She was going to bath and relax and maybe do some studying for her next exams. She thought of Gideon. What was wrong with the boy? She knew that he had been through a terrible experience, but there was something about him that was at times . . . menacing. She liked her job, liked helping people, and she had a lot of patience. She hardly ever became ruffled by the people she had to deal with in the ward. And yet, in Gideon's case, she felt a strange antagonism. Did he deliberately try to provoke her, staring with those heavy-lidded eyes of his? That morning he had started to talk. If only she had been able to hear what he had said, but she realised now, as she walked along the lonely path, that she had not been intended to hear. He had been speaking to himself, not answering her. And she thought again of the monotonous flow of unknown words. Then for the rest of the day he had been as silent as before. Most of the time he had ignored her existence almost completely. She felt that she wanted to shake him, to release herself from his staring eyes. Yet she pushed that angry thought aside. That wasn't the right way to deal with a patient.

'He'll talk tomorrow,' she thought to herself. She was determined to break through the hostile barrier which he had erected around himself. 'Yes, tomorrow,' she said.

In the distance, she heard again the urgent barking of a dog. Then it was taken up by another. The blended sound seemed eerie as she walked along between the shading bushes.

Nurse Simpson walked on more quickly. The noise of barking had ceased for a moment, only to rise again, louder than before. But she refused to think of it, refused to listen to the sound.

Dogs. She loathed them. When other people stroked

them, or made a fuss of them, she stepped back, keeping her distance. She hated them to be close. The sight of the panting tongue dripping with saliva, the pungent smell. Once, when she was a child, something awful had happened, something which she never allowed herself to think of. She walked on even more quickly, practically running down the path. Then, as if in mockery of her fears, she heard a dog barking again. It was very loud and very close. She stood still on the path, unable to go forward. In front of her the path twisted out of sight between huge banks of bushes. What if . . .? What if there *was* a dog waiting for her around that corner? It might be huge, with its lips drawn back, with great bared teeth and white bulbous eyes.

She forced back the tears. 'This is silly,' she said to herself, because the picture of the waiting dog on the path ahead was only a projection of her old memory. 'It can't happen,' she said to herself. Unwillingly, she submitted to the encroaching memory of her early experience. She tried to keep it away from her thoughts but she could not. The noise of the barking dogs, and somehow the thought of Gideon's piercing eyes, brought it all back. She had been six years old. Dressed in a new blue dress, she had waited at the front gate for her father to come home. They had been going out somewhere, she couldn't remember where. She had waited for a long time and still he had not come, so she had stepped out of the garden and on to the pavement beyond. Then, it had happened. Behind her she had heard a furious barking and, turning round quickly, she had been confronted by a dog bigger than she had ever seen. A great dane, taller than she was. Its mouth was open and it came right up to her. It licked her face. She could see into its open mouth, the pointed teeth hung with strands of saliva, the red and cavernous interior of the throat.

Standing on the path between the rhododendrons she

heard the barking even closer to her. But she wasn't a child any more. Such things ought not to be frightening. She opened her eyes and took a step forward. Then, glancing over her shoulder, she saw a sight which froze her blood to ice.

A pack. Brindle and black hair, very coarse. Yellow unblinking eyes. Eyes which met hers, which were fastened on hers. As she backed away *they* edged forward. When she stopped *they* stopped. Mouths open. White jagged teeth, hanging tongues. Everything about them that she feared.

Then, led by the huge brute at the front of the pack, they charged forward, their jaws snapping towards her, their eyes angry with blood lust.

With a shriek of horror she turned and fled. 'This can't be happening,' she thought. 'Not in the park. It isn't possible.' But she could hear them pursuing her, baying like wolves who were hunting down a victim. Her feet pounded on the path as she ran in wild fear.

Once, when she looked behind her, she saw that they were gaining on her, getting closer. She had a brief sight of their muzzles. The pointed ugly snouts. Sniffing nostrils and drawn-back lips. Such white sharp teeth, waiting to tear her flesh.

She was crying, the tears of terror running out of her eyes as she moved. The leaves of the bushes whipped against her face. Behind her were the persistent, chasing hounds. The sound of their huge black pads echoed softly on the stone pathway.

'Don't touch me!' The words in her head, confused, confusing, like the voice of some other person calling out. 'I'll never be able to go fast enough,' she thought. 'They'll catch me.'

They were at her heels now. One or two of them snapped at her feet in the flimsy open sandals. She felt their hot breath on her skin. From their throats came a horrible rasping growl. They were after her blood.

A scream of terror rose up in her. She must run, she must get away. She broke out from the bushes on to a wide stretch of grass. One of the dogs was running beside her, leaping as it went, coming close to her face. She saw its leering mouth. There was cruelty in the mouth. It taunted her with a savage smile.

Then, a strap on one of her sandals broke and she tripped and fell full-length on the grass. She was immediately surrounded by the pack. Ugly faces, bearing down upon her, seeming to pin her to the ground. Teeth pulled at her clothes. Ribbons of material flew into the air like strips of torn-off flesh. She could feel their oily tongues on her skin.

Almost fainting, she twisted and turned on the grass. A few more seconds and they would begin to devour her. Their faces were even closer now and she saw the threat in their glinting eyes. She thought of her limbs, torn one from the other, shared out amongst the pack. She saw the jagged edges of her own flesh as it was ripped from the bone, the white bones snapped and broken between the teeth of the dogs and then licked clean. She saw the cascade of hot blood seeping into the grass. And every time one of them drew its tongue along her skin she wondered if the lick would become the first bite, if the teeth would close together on her flesh and tear out a piece of her. She lay on the ground in an agony of paralysis. Why didn't anyone come to help her? There must be people about. There must be. But no one came.

'I must get away,' she thought. Away from the open mouths and the fetid stench of their breath. Overcoming the deadening sense of horror, she forced herself to roll over. Then, leaping to her feet, she began to run.

They were after her immediately, bounding and jumping as if they knew that it was impossible for her to escape. They would wear her down, wear the life out of her. Then, when she was too tired to run any more, they would tear her to pieces, drink her blood. The vomit rose in her throat as she ran. They were going to kill her. She wouldn't be able to get free of them.

She fled like a wild and hunted thing, across the grass. Before her was the north gate. She almost cried in relief when she saw it looming up before her. If only she could get there. There would be people on the street. If she could get to the gate, and beyond it, she would be safe.

With a tremendous spurt of speed she raced across the last few yards of grass. All her energy, all her strength, were forced into that last violent flight.

She was level with the gates. The road ahead of her was a steady stream of fast flowing traffic. The dogs were licking at her elbows now, and a voracious howl was rising out of them. In her blind terror she ran out of the gates and across the pavement and on to the road.

The bus driver had no chance to stop. Before him was this wild and flying girl. He automatically braked as hard as he could, but it was too late. Her body was tossed up into the air, and the people on the bus cried out as her white face was thrown up against the window and then disappeared. She lay cracked and broken on the road.

'What made her run out like that?' the bus conductor was saying.

Everybody asked the question, but there was no answer to be found.

10

Theresa was sitting on the couch in the little sitting-room of the flat which Phil had found for her. 'I feel restless,' she said. 'I don't know why, exactly.'

Phil was in the adjoining kitchenette making a cup of coffee. 'Did you sleep all right?' he asked, 'or did it feel strange being on your own here?'

'Oh, I slept fine,' she said. 'And I like being here. It's almost like a little doll's house. Yes, it's very comfortable,' she added, patting the cushions on the couch beside her.

'It will take you a long while to get over what's happened, I should think,' Phil said, stirring the milk into the cups. 'I think you've made an amazing recovery, considering.'

'When I was first in the hospital I was just sad. Now I'm becoming angry. Such a stupid accident. How on earth did it happen?'

'I've been asking myself the same thing,' Phil said, coming into the room with the two cups. 'And the police don't know either. They've scoured the remains of the house from top to bottom, apparently. And there's no evidence of anything.'

'They came and questioned me at the hospital,' Theresa told him. 'But I couldn't tell them anything.'

'They questioned me too,' Phil said. 'I had a long talk with the inspector. He and the accident investigator have looked into every possible cause. They said it seemed like spontaneous combustion. They couldn't understand it at all.'

'I think that's what is making me feel uneasy. Not

knowing the cause. It's a nightmare to me.'

'Come on, drink your coffee,' Phil said, handing her the cup.

She sighed, and tears came into her eyes. 'I just can't adjust to the fact that mum and dad are dead.'

Phil sat down beside her on the couch and put his arm round her. 'I know it's hard,' he said.

'Damn,' Theresa said. She put the cup down on the low coffee table. 'Damn,' she said again. The tears were streaming from her eyes and she could not stop them. 'I'm sorry, Phil. I don't mean to upset you by letting you see me like this. I don't want to cry, but I really can't help it.'

He leaned over and kissed her face. 'Don't worry about that,' he said. 'It's better to cry than to suppress your feelings. You must cry if you need to.'

For a few moments she continued to sob. 'I feel such a fool,' she told him.

'But it's understandable,' he said to her. 'I'd be crying if it had happened to me.'

'I keep seeing their faces,' she said. 'At the window. And I keep thinking, "Perhaps I could have done something." '

'You mustn't think like that,' Phil said. 'There was nothing you could do.'

Theresa squinted her eyes. The tears had stopped flowing and she wiped her face with a handkerchief. 'Have the police mentioned to you that they suspect anything?' she asked Phil in a low voice.

'Not exactly,' Phil said. 'It's just that it's an unlikely sort of accident, and they've checked the wiring and all the electrical stuff. There were no paraffin heaters or anything . . .' His voice trailed off.

'I suppose it's not possible,' Theresa said. 'No one would start a fire like that. And anyway, there would be traces, wouldn't there?' She looked at Phil uneasily.

'There's usually evidence of something,' Phil said.

'Whether it is an accident or arson. I think that's what's mystifying them. They can't find anything.'

'Let's go out,' Theresa said suddenly.

Phil's face brightened. 'That's a good idea,' he said. 'It's a lovely day. Where would you like to go? Shall we go out for a picnic somewhere?' And then he looked at her. She wasn't smiling, but sitting tightly on the couch and looking grim. His face fell. 'What's the matter?' he asked.

'I want to go back to the old house. I want to see it.' There was determination in her voice.

'But what's the point of that? It will only bring back the bad memories more vividly than ever. There's nothing you can do, Theresa. You'll just have to accept it. I'm sorry, I'm not trying to be unkind, but you will. It's over now. Nothing is going to bring your mum and dad back. Wouldn't it be better to forget all about it? I don't mean that you should forget *them*, but you've got yourself to think of, and Gideon. You can't let yourself go to pieces. You mustn't go there again, Theresa. Please.' He reached out his hand towards her.

'It's true what you say,' she agreed, 'but still . . . Somehow, it doesn't feel as if it is over.' She looked at Phil strangely. 'It feels as if there's more to come. I can't explain it to you. I don't even know what I mean myself. It's just a weird feeling that I have. I've got to go back there, honestly I have. I'm not being morbid.' Her eyes clouded over again and one or two tears ran down her cheeks. 'I don't even want to go. I know it will be upsetting. But I must. I've got to see. Please try to understand, Phil. I must look at the place.'

He nodded gloomily. 'All right,' he said. 'Perhaps when you've been there you will be able to put all this out of your head.' He sighed. 'But it will be hard, you know. The place is in a terrible state.' He shook his head.

'You've been there?' she asked him.

'Yes.' His voice was low. 'I didn't tell you before. I

thought it would only make you brood more. I went back to see if there was anything that could be saved.'

'And was there?' she asked, but she already knew the answer. When he shook his head he confirmed her worst fears.

They stood at the gate of the driveway which led to the house.

'You see what I meant,' Phil said. 'Everything was destroyed, everything burnt out.'

They looked at the ruins of the house. The roof had collapsed inwards and most of the walls had cracked in the heat and tumbled down, scattering charred brick over the ground. There was no evidence of the window where Theresa's parents had stood on that fateful night. Only the central chimney-stack remained intact.

'Do you want to see more?' Phil asked her gently.

Theresa nodded mutely and pushed open the gate.

'Don't go in,' Phil said, but she was already walking forward, and so he followed her.

'This is where I stood with Mrs MacKenzie,' Theresa said in a flat and unnaturally quiet voice. She glanced up to where the window had been. Now it was just a gap in the brickwork where the blue sky showed through.

Standing there in front of the burnt-out ruin of the house Theresa swayed slightly on her feet, as though she was going to faint. Phil took hold of her arm and steadied her.

'Haven't you seen enough?' he asked. 'This isn't doing you any good, you know.'

Theresa walked forward to where the front door had been. A pile of ash, nothing more. 'I was happy here,' she whispered, kneeling down and touching the ash with her fingers. 'I can't believe it's all a part of the past now.'

Phil lifted her up. Little columns of dust rose from the ashes when they moved. Theresa took a step inside. She was standing in what had once been the hall.

'That's where the stairs were,' she said. 'Do you remember?'

They both looked up, trying to picture how it had been. But already it was hard to remember exactly, even though only two weeks had passed. The exact colour of the paper, the precise angle of the stairs themselves, and the width of each tread. The details of all those things were hard to capture.

'There used to be a print of the sea hanging on that wall above the stairs,' Theresa said sadly, 'and do you know, I can't recall now whether the sea was green or grey. Yet that picture was part of my life. I always noticed it when I went up the stairs.'

'Come away,' Phil said to her, and this time he took her by the hand and led her out of the eerie enclosure.

Theresa stumbled away from the dilapidated ruin. 'I don't know why I came,' she said. 'I think I'm going to be sick.'

'Breathe deeply,' Phil told her. He was walking her up and down the path.

'Do you remember that last day?' Theresa sobbed. 'We were together here in the garden. Wasn't it beautiful? Can we go back and look at everything just this once?'

They walked hand in hand across the already overgrown grass at the side of the house, then across the lawn.

'It's growing so fast,' Theresa said. 'There's no one to cut it.' She had a sudden sharp memory of her father. Sunday afternoons. The noise of the motor mower, and the sweet smell of fresh-cut grass. 'Why did it happen?' she cried. 'Why?'

They were on the path that led to the little ornamental pool. Between the slabs of stone the weeds were already pushing up. Then they stood side by side looking down at the water.

Suddenly they both shrank back. Caught among the

weeds at the edge of the pond were the skeletal bones of dead fish. White and motionless they floated on the grey-brown water.

'Let's get away,' Theresa said. 'Let's get away.'

11

Mrs MacKenzie held the telephone tightly in her hand. 'That would be very nice, Theresa,' she said. 'I'll get a tea ready for you.' She nodded her head as if she was already planning it. 'No, no,' she interrupted. 'It's no trouble really. I'd like to do it, I want to. It will be lovely to see you again.' She listened to the voice at the other end of the line. 'All right, then, in about an hour. Yes, I'll be here.' She laughed. 'I hardly ever go out, my dear. Bye-bye for the moment, then.'

She put down the black receiver and stood by the table, looking out of the window at the tiny garden in front of the cottage. She supposed she was lucky that her brother had had this place. At least she'd had somewhere to go. It was lonely, though, because he was away on business for a month and she couldn't help feeling a bit depressed. She'd never been on her own before and, somehow, cleaning the house and cooking just for yourself didn't seem the same. She had been a housekeeper most of her life. Now she had shrunk back into a tired old age. Perhaps it would be different when her brother came home. He was a widower, and had always wanted her to go and live with him. She had always refused. She liked being with families where there were children. It made her feel young.

For a while she stood there listlessly, thinking of when she had first had a job with a family. She couldn't quite recall their name, but in the first year she had been there the lady had had a baby. Mrs MacKenzie smiled, flushed with the memory. A pretty little thing, it was. A girl. She racked her brains. Emily, was it, or Emma? She couldn't remember. She wondered what had happened to that little girl. She'd be a grown woman by now, of course. Then there was . . .

Mrs MacKenzie shook herself out of her reverie. 'This will never do,' she said out loud. 'Mooning around here. I'd better get cracking. I think I'll bake some little tarts. There's a bit of ham left. I'll make some sandwiches.'

And for the next hour she felt happy again, relaxed and needed. She liked being of use to somebody. While she worked she began to think of the future. Perhaps when Theresa got married to Mr Carson – 'Phil', he had told her to call him, but she didn't like to – perhaps then they would get a big house and would need a housekeeper. She would look after them. And later Theresa would have children . . . The daydreams stretched out until Mrs MacKenzie, opening the oven door, burnt her fingers on the hot tray. 'There,' she said. 'That's for not thinking of what you're doing.' She ran her hand under the cold tap. 'You silly old thing,' she scolded herself.

When the doorbell rang the table was laid with a spread of food, enough for ten. She surveyed it with some pride and then went to open the door. 'Oh, Theresa,' she said, as soon as she saw her. 'Whatever did happen to your hair?' The old woman threw up her arms in horror. 'Such pretty hair you had.' She gathered Theresa up in her arms and embraced her. 'Come in, my dear,' she said. 'Come in.'

'It's lovely to see you,' Theresa said quietly. 'I had to have my hair cut. It was burnt. But it will grow again, just as before.'

'I would have come to see you at the hospital,' Mrs MacKenzie said. 'But it's such a long way from here, and I don't like going on those buses. Come on in, Mr Carson,' she said. 'Don't stand there by the door.'

Phil grinned sheepishly. It always embarrassed him when she called him 'Mr Carson'.

'I've got a nice tea ready for you – not too much, nothing special. You didn't give me enough time.' She led the way into the little dining-room where the tea was laid.

'We've been to the old house,' Theresa said.

'Tch, tch, tch. Why ever did you want to do that?' Mrs MacKenzie scolded. 'It will only upset you going back there.'

'That's what I told her,' Phil said.

'There's something not right, I can feel it.' Theresa's voice was insistent.

'Sh. There's no use brooding about what's happened,' Mrs MacKenzie told her. 'It was a terrible thing. Terrible. But we've got to go on, haven't we.'

She ushered the two of them into chairs at the dining-table.

'What an enormous spread,' Phil said.

Mrs MacKenzie smiled at him, gratified. 'I've just got to make the tea,' she said.

During the meal Mrs MacKenzie and Phil kept up a light conversation, trying to draw Theresa from time to time, but unsuccessfully. They both looked at her anxiously, wishing that there was something that they could do. Theresa sat rather dejectedly between them, not eating very much and looking very dismal. She stared down disconsolately at the plate in front of her. Once or twice, not wanting to seem ungrateful, she took a sandwich from a plate, or helped herself to a biscuit.

They had been sitting there for about half an hour when they were disturbed by strange noises in the chimney-breast.

'What on earth is it?' Mrs MacKenzie asked.

Desperate scratching noises, and occasionally a wild

squawking. Into the grate fell a steady drift of soot.

'I think it's a bird trapped in the chimney,' Phil said. He and Theresa went over to the fireplace, but Mrs MacKenzie hung back, her face pale.

'It's not a bird,' the old woman said, putting her hand to her throat as though for protection.

The soot was accompanied now by wisps of straw and fibrous-looking twistings of hair.

'Not a bird,' Mrs MacKenzie muttered again.

'Isn't there anything we can do to help it?' Theresa asked Phil.

Phil shrugged his shoulders. 'We'll never get to it,' he said. He peered up into the chimney but he could see nothing. 'This often happens at this time of year,' he said.

'Why doesn't it just fly up?' Theresa was distraught.

'Gets in a sort of panic, I suppose,' Phil answered. He knelt down again to look into the chimney.

Suddenly, with a flurry of feathers and soot, the bird crashed down into the grate. It lay there dazed for a moment and then flew wildly out into the room.

'It's a starling,' Phil said, noting the bluish flecks on its black feathers.

The three of them were in a kind of shock as the bird careered crazily about the room. Sometimes it flew straight at a wall, as if it would smash its way through. Then it sank down on to the floor, only to rise again and continue the wild fluttering.

'It will hurt itself,' Theresa cried out.

The bird was flying from one side of the room to the other, searching desperately for a way out. It landed on the dining-table, leaving a black smear of soot on the white cloth.

Mrs MacKenzie's mouth was open and she stared at it in horror, unable to move. She was clinging to the side of the table.

Then the starling was off again, dizzily circling the

room, bumping into objects, sometimes disappearing from sight behind the sideboard or one of the chairs. Once, it flew straight at Theresa's face. She lifted up her hand, but it veered off at the last moment.

'Open the window, Mrs MacKenzie,' Phil called, 'and I'll open the door.'

She did not respond, and when they looked at the old lady they found that she could neither speak nor move. Her lips were trembling and her face was ashen.

Theresa ran across the room and pushed open the casement, which was rather stiff and unyielding but finally moved to her touch. 'It's open,' she called out to Phil.

'Come over this side,' he said. 'We'll try and head it towards the open window.'

They stood by the wall and waved their hands, but that only increased the bird's confusion. It was hysterical with fear and did not seem to recognise that the window was open and that it could escape. Again and again it flew at the wall in unthinking repetition. Blind and crazed, it smashed its tiny body against the plaster.

'Why doesn't it fly out?' Theresa screamed, hating the bird for its dazed stupidity. 'The window's open. Why doesn't it just go?'

Phil had opened the door, and the front door too, thinking that if it flew into the hall it might escape that way.

But no. It seemed almost self-destructive in its resistance to their efforts. It continued to batter itself against the wall and the ceiling, so that its feathers came out and drifted slowly to the floor. Then, in one last frantic effort, it circled the room, ever faster, ever more frenzied, finally flinging itself against the closed part of the window. It fell back from the window-sill to the floor with its wing tips fluttering.

There was silence for a second in the room, then

Theresa ran across and gathered it into her hands. As she did so, Mrs MacKenzie let out a little cry of horror.

'Is it dead?' Phil asked, coming over to Theresa's side.

She shook her head.'No, I can feel its heart beating. It's beating so fast. It must have been petrified.'

'If we put it in the garden and lay it in the sun it might recover,' Phil said.

They took it out and left it on a patch of grass. Then they went back inside and watched from the window. After a minute they saw it jerk its head up and then, unbelievably, it hopped up, ruffled and then smoothed its feathers, and flew away as if nothing had happened. They turned back into the room. Mrs MacKenzie was still sitting rigidly by the table.

Theresa went over and put her arm round the old lady's shoulders. 'Are you all right, Mrs MacKenzie?' she asked.

'I hate them,' Mrs MacKenzie said with a shudder. 'My granny used to tell me they peck your eyes out when they go mad like that. Thank God you were here.'

'Of course they don't,' Theresa told her. 'And anyway, it's gone now.'

But it took them a long time to console her. The experience had turned her skin grey and coarse, which made her look older. When she took the cup of tea that Theresa made for her, her hand was trembling and the cup rattled in the saucer.

'I hate them,' she kept repeating.

12

There was a subdued air in the ward. Everyone had heard about Nurse Simpson's accident. It made them depressed. Any news of death was oppressive in the closely confined atmosphere, but Nurse Simpson had been a particular favourite. They sat around in the day-room with long faces. There was hardly any talk. From time to time, the nurses, drawing on their professional reserves, tried to cheer the patients up, but the news of the death was heavy, and there was little response.

'Come on, Robert,' one of the nurses said. 'Aren't you going to play table tennis today?'

The man was sitting on the floor with a white ball in his hand. 'I don't feel like it,' he muttered.

The weather continued fine, the sun shining brightly, but no one ventured out into the garden. One or two of the men sat huddled deep in armchairs, crying gently like children, the tears slipping down their faces.

It was early afternoon. Lunch had been a quiet and dismal affair, the silence broken only by the scraping of spoons and the clatter of dishes as they were piled neatly into stacks at the end of the meal.

Gideon sat in the chair by the window, looking out across the grass. In the deserted gardens birds settled on the branches and hopped confidently down on to the lawn, pecking greedily for worms or at crumbs of food which had been dropped there.

The door to the day-room opened and a nurse came in carrying a jug of orange juice and a plate of biscuits. 'Come on,' she called. 'It's five o'clock. Time for juice.' But no one rushed over to her as they normally did. Their movements when they got out of their chairs were slow and heavy and apathetic.

Gideon stared out of the window at the grass, the hedge, the line of trees. Beyond the garden was the lake. He thought for a moment, of the garden around the house where he had once lived – the burnt house. In the garden was a long path which led to the ornamental pond. Then he thought of Theresa.

A flock of starlings skittered down from the hedge to the lawn and settled like dark leaves on the grass, pecking with sharp beaks at the earth. Through the glass he could hear their ugly, chattering noise.

'Come on, Gideon,' the nurse called over.

'He's watching the birds,' Williams said from the other side of the room.

Gideon went across and took his glass of juice, and when he returned to his chair Williams was there, standing beside it. When Gideon sat down Williams also sat, drawing up another chair from a little way off.

Suddenly Williams banged on the window and the birds flew off, rising into the sky like a black cloud. He gave a little laugh and then turned to look at Gideon, his head on one side.

Gideon sipped at the glass in his hand, apparently unaware of Williams' presence.

'What are you looking at?' Williams asked. 'Why do you keep looking out of the window? There's no one there. No one's going out there today. And she's not there. She's dead, you know.'

Williams hung forward over his chair. There was a listlessness in his pale, thin body, as though the flesh was hardly supported by the gaunt bone structure. He kept crossing and uncrossing his legs, constantly rubbing his hands together as though he would wipe them clean. In his limp white face his eyes burnt with a feverish restlessness. He was never still, always moving, looking around him as if to make sure that he was not being overheard. Now he leant forward to Gideon confidentially. 'You didn't like her, did you,' he said. 'I didn't like her. She was in it with the doctor. They tried to kill me, you know.' A hurt look flashed across his face. 'And then they lied about things.' A knowing look entered the burning eyes. 'I pretended to like her, and perhaps in a kind of way I did. Sometimes I did. She liked *me* you know.' His face took on a certain meanness. 'But she didn't like you. I could tell. She was trying to get you, like she was trying to get me. I heard her talking to the sister when you first came. I heard her.' Then suddenly Williams' eyes swelled with tears. 'She's dead. I didn't think they'd get *her*. I thought it was only me they wanted.' His voice lowered. 'It's my fault, you know. I should have warned her.'

For a moment he sat there, the tears running down his face and on to his hand. And for that instant he did not move. He looked at the spots of water that had landed on his skin as if they were drops of rain, as if they had no connection with him at all. Then, furiously and with a grimace of distaste, he wiped them away.

'I'm getting better. They don't believe me, but I am. That's why I didn't like her. Because she didn't believe me. You ought to believe people when they tell you something. I told her I was getting better and she just nodded and smiled, and I could tell that she thought I was lying. And then I fell over.' He glanced across at Gideon, remembering the pain in his head, the way the world had gone black, the sight of the grass very close to his face. He looked suspicious. 'You saw me, didn't you,' he said. 'You were watching through this window – this very window. She didn't like you,' he said. Then his body stiffened and took on a more angular look. 'Nobody likes you, do they. I heard her talking to the sister. There was a big fire, and everybody died. Now she's dead.'

Suddenly Gideon looked coldly into Williams' face. 'Be

quiet,' he whispered through his teeth. 'You don't know what you're talking about. You're mad.' Then Gideon glanced around the room. No one had seen him speak. They'd never believe it if Williams told them.

'You're mad,' he said again.

Williams was staring at him with his mouth wide open. There was a hurt look in his eyes. 'You mustn't say things like that,' he said. 'I'll be your friend. I don't mind about the fire. Whatever happened, I don't mind. Only, you mustn't say bad things about me.'

'It's true,' Gideon said. 'You're not getting better. You're getting worse. You had a fit yesterday, didn't you? Remember the pain inside your head, like a hot wire in the blackness?'

Williams was holding his head with both his hands. 'How do you know what it was like?' he said in a muffled voice. He turned away from Gideon and looked out of the window. He was trying, in his confused mind, to put things together, to make some sort of order. 'She didn't like you,' he said to himself. 'And you didn't like her.' Then, suddenly, out loud, he said, 'There was a fire and everyone died.' His voice was loud and echoed round the room.

A nurse hastily came across to them. 'Anything the matter, Mr Williams? Everything all right? Not getting excited, are we?'

'I'm talking to Gideon,' he said sulkily. 'About the fire.'

The nurse frowned. 'That's very naughty of you,' she said. 'You mustn't talk about things like that. Come on now. You come with me.'

A look of terror passed into Williams' eyes. 'What are you going to do? Where are you taking me?'

'Now don't be silly,' she said, getting exasperated. 'You come over and sit with me at the table. You can talk to me for a little while.'

Williams sat stubbornly in his chair, refusing to move.

'He started it,' he said meaninglessly, like a child who feels he is being wrongly accused.

'Come along now,' the nurse said sternly, and Williams' resistance crumbled. He got up and ambled over to the table. The nurse leant over Gideon's shoulder. 'Everything all right, Gideon?' she asked.

He did not look at her. She was insignificant.

'You mustn't let Mr Williams upset you. He doesn't mean any harm.' When Gideon didn't respond she turned and followed Williams across to the table.

Gideon was angry. He wanted to get out of here, but Theresa did not come. He had tried to concentrate on her, to force her to come to him, but somehow whenever he thought of her there was a veil in his mind which he could not break through. He was getting to loathe it in this place. First there was that Nurse Simpson, and now there was Williams. Always talking, always asking questions. Why didn't they leave him alone? To be alone, that was what he wanted, and yet . . . He had never been alone before, not really alone. There had always been somebody there. His mother, or his father. No! He closed his mind to the thought of them. That was childish. To think of them was weak, and he wouldn't do it. He had to be strong. Theresa *would* come. Tomorrow, the doctor had said. She'd be coming tomorrow. And when she came he would talk to her normally, as if everything was all right, and then they'd let him go home. There was something twisting at the back of his mind, something hot and painful. Flames and smoke, trying to choke him. But he pushed them away from him, encased them in a dark box inside his mind. He could control the fire.

Suddenly there was a commotion from the nurse's desk, and Gideon looked over sharply. It was Williams again. Gideon clenched his teeth.

Williams was standing by the nurse's desk waving his hands and shouting out in a high and uncontrolled voice.

'He *did* speak to me, he *did* speak to me. Nobody believes anything.' He was stamping his feet in fury. 'Why don't you believe me?'

'What did he say, then?' the nurse asked quietly. 'Be quiet now, and tell me that.'

Gideon was listening carefully.

'I'm not going to tell you,' Williams said. 'I'm not going to tell you. You won't believe me, anyway, will you? But he did speak to me. We were talking about the fire. And he said horrible things to me.'

'Can you remember what they were?' the nurse asked placatingly.

'And now *she's* dead.' Williams was crying and shouting.

The sister came in, and she and the nurse led Williams out of the day-room.

'He's upset,' the nurse said. 'He keeps talking about Nurse Simpson. I knew there would be trouble here today.'

They went through the door, and Gideon could hear him screaming still, from the corridor beyond.

13

It was very quiet in the dormitory. Gideon lay wide-awake, looking at the silver light of the moon on the window, and sometimes glancing at the empty bed opposite. They had moved Williams into the empty cubicle.

'So he won't keep you awake,' a nurse explained.

It was three o'clock in the morning. The only sound was the rustle of paper as the night nurse turned over a page of the book she was reading. Everyone was quiet.

Gideon got out of bed and put on a dressing-gown. The night nurse looked up as he walked past her.

'Going to the bathroom?' she asked and, expecting no answer, assumed that that was the case. She went back to her book.

He walked the full length of the room then glanced over his shoulder. There was no one looking, so he slipped into the cubicle where Williams was sleeping. He stood by the side of the bed and stared down at the thin pale face.

'Wake up,' he whispered.

Slowly, Williams opened his eyes. Then, when he saw Gideon, he was startled and came instantly awake. He was about to call out, but his voice was stifled by a glare from Gideon. Like a rabbit held transfixed by the hypnotic eyes of a snake, he sat paralysed on the bed.

'I warned you,' Gideon whispered. His voice was cold and hard, like a thin steel thread. 'I told you to keep quiet, not to say anything. You're making trouble for me.'

Williams stared at him dumbfounded. His head was spinning with the sedative they had given him but he could see Gideon sharply and clearly. He was sure that he wasn't dreaming, that Gideon was really there, watching him from the shadows. He wanted to scream, he wanted to cry out, but he could not. His voice was trapped inside his throat. Then he forced himself to speak. 'I won't,' he whispered. 'I won't talk about anything.'

'You don't know how to be quiet,' Gideon said scornfully.

Williams hunched up his thin body, drawing away from the cruel words.

'You're mad, and you talk too much.' Gideon's voice was like a whip, goading, and flicking into the weak mind. 'Remember the sharp pain? That's what you deserve. To be always in pain.'

'Why don't you leave me alone?' Williams pleaded.

'What do you want?' Then his eyes widened, the whites appearing to bulge and lift up the irises to the corners. 'You want to kill me, don't you? You're in it. I know you are. That's why you hate me. It's because of the fire.'

Gideon's face darkened in a scowl. 'You fool,' he said.

'I know what happened,' Williams murmured, and suddenly his eyes shone with a clear light. 'I know what happened. I can see you. It's all dark. Then the light comes. You are standing here.' He leant forward in his bed, the striped pyjamas hanging loosely on his bony body. 'They said there was a fire.' He squinted as though he could smell the smoke and see the flames.

'What do you know?' Gideon sneered.

Williams' white face stared out into the darkness. He was shaking. It was as if he knew in his confused and disordered mind that Gideon was responsible for the fire. He, in his madness, had hit upon what no one else had considered. He pictured Gideon with a flaming torch setting fire to the buildings of the hospital, saw the patients dying in their burning beds.

'Don't set light to me,' he whimpered. 'I won't tell.' He looked down at the boy who stood at the end of his bed, and shook his head. There was so much confusion. Who was it standing here? He didn't really know. A whirl of gossip that he had overheard and a few random facts tumbled around inside his head, fragmented and insubstantial. Little was real to him, except a spreading wave of fear, fear that was always inside him but was now growing.

'I know . . .' he began, but the words were too big for his mouth, so that it opened and closed, fumbling with the forms that he was trying to frame. 'She died.' He started to cry. Someone had died. He knew that. In his head there were flames and blood and death, but he couldn't sort them out. 'I know . . .' The words trailed off.

Gideon drew in his breath, an ugly, slow, inhalation. 'You will be quiet,' he whispered.

For a long time he stood there watching Williams, his eyes narrow and glinting with purpose.

Williams writhed under the intensity, then he let out a groan.

Nodding to himself Gideon turned stiffly and stepped out of the shadow. He walked slowly back to his own cubicle.

The night nurse looked up, smiled, and then went back to her reading. She had not heard Williams' whispered pleas and Gideon's harsh retorts. All was quiet tonight, there was no disturbance.

Williams crawled out of his bed, looking around him with frightened eyes. Beads of sweat ran down his forehead. He must get away. They were coming to get him. And inside him he could feel the sharp hot pain. It tore at his stomach and twisted like a razored edge into his mind. Everyone was against him. He began to sob, and pulling himself across the floor he curled up in the corner by the wall. Gideon had gone but Williams could see him still. The boy was standing there with eyes of fire. A cold flame in his eyes penetrated into the deepest recesses of Williams' unconscious.

'*Go away*,' Williams screamed out.

The night nurse looked up. At first she didn't know where the cry came from. Perhaps it was a patient calling out in his sleep. They often did that. Then it came again.

'Don't hurt me! Go away!'

She saw Williams trembling in the shadows. His knees were drawn up to his chest and he was hugging them tightly with his arms, rocking backwards and forwards.

'Mr Williams,' she called out in a loud whisper. 'Mr Williams. Go back to bed.' She stood up from the desk, closing the book abruptly.

Williams stared at her. She was all in white. From the

pocket of her uniform he could see a steel watch hanging down. She was coming to get him. He knew that she would drag him back, drag him by the throat, her clean white fingers tearing their nails into him. Red fingernails. Blood red. 'I'm frightened,' he whimpered. He wanted nothing but to be left alone, yet he knew that they would not allow him his peace.

The nurse was standing beside him. She spoke quietly and gently, but to Williams the voice was charged with cold and hostile authority. He pushed her away and closed his eyes. Blood-red knives, sharp and curved down, touching with stiletto points the watery surface of his eyes. He could feel them. They wanted to blind him. They wanted him to suffer. He flailed out with his arms, and the nurse was knocked sideways.

Scrambling away, she made her way over to her desk and pressed the alarm button. She heard its jangling echo in the distant orderly room. The orderlies would soon be running down the stairs to help her. When she looked back to the cubicle she saw that Williams had not moved. He was crouched in rigid immobility, staring ahead, the saliva running down his chin, his teeth grinding together.

He opened his mouth and screamed, the foam coating itself around his lips. Then, lifting his head and looking up at the ceiling as though he were about to be attacked by a vast and implacable enemy, he bayed in fear.

'Be quiet,' the nurse said sternly. 'You'll wake the others.'

But everyone else was already awake. They sat up in their beds or stood in their pyjamas looking across at Williams. Only Gideon remained where he was, staring into the darkness.

Williams screamed like an animal in a trap. The thin, keening sound echoed against the ceiling and the bare painted walls.

The two orderlies on night duty came running through

the doors of the dormitory.

'There they are,' thought Williams. 'They're coming!' He could see them, a crowd of them. They were coming towards him. His greatest fear was that he would one day be taken and torn to pieces. They would punch him and kick him, and he would feel fingernails tearing away strips of his flesh. He began to bang the back of his head against the wall behind him, a slow rhythmical movement that jarred the bones of his neck. They mustn't get hold of him.

One of the orderlies reached out a hand.

'Don't kill me,' Williams shouted.

'Calm down now.' The orderly's voice was impatient. 'Don't be silly.'

But Williams hardly heard him. His glazed eye saw a black and hostile world and his ears were blocked to reason.

'Mr Williams,' the nurse pleaded. She could see the abject terror in his eyes and was frightened for him. 'I'll call the duty doctor,' she said to the orderly.

The second orderly had prepared a syringe at the nurse's desk, a strong sedative, but as he approached, Williams slid across the floor between the two advancing men and scrambled away. They chased after him.

Williams' mind was dominated by the thought of escaping them. It was racked by fear and tormented by the vision of what they would do to him. He could almost feel their thumbs upon his eyes, their knives upon his body. He had seen the silver glint of the sharp needle. *They want to destroy me*, he thought.

But there was a way to elude them, all of them. They had not thought of it but *he* had. Yes, he would escape from them, and also from what was even more terrifying: that boy with his staring eyes. He would elude him as well.

'Gideon,' he shouted, his voice distorted by the foaming saliva in his mouth.

He jumped to his feet and ran the full length of the dormitory.

'There's nothing to be afraid of.' The orderly's voice. Far off. Distant.

A lie. Williams heard, and knew. They were trying to trick him.

He reached the end wall. There was a window. He stretched out his arm and thrust it through the glass. A sharp crack, and the long shards flew out, leaving an irregular star-shaped hole.

'Mr Williams!' The nurse screamed his name.

Yes. He could prevent them from hurting him. He leant forward and dragged his throat across a jagged splinter. He felt the skin open. It was like a whisper of silk that was being stroked. No pain. A strange pleasure. The blood ran slowly down the glass.

Williams stared forward. It was dark out there. Above him there were one or two stars and in the distance, street lights. There would be no more pain.

The orderlies stood shocked and hesitant beside him, afraid to move him for fear of making the damage worse. 'Get the doctor,' one of them cried out.

The long spear of glass went into his throat as he slipped forward. He felt the spurt of blood pulsing out of him.

No more. They wouldn't come after him any more. Something deep in his mind moved, a subterranean flicker, the power of an invidious insistence. Gideon.

The blood was gurgling in his throat as he tried to gulp in breath. The word he was trying to say was lost as his body shuddered into death and the darkness of the night swamped down into his head. His eyes glazed over and he could see no more. Throughout the dimly lit ward there was the noise of sobbing and screaming, but Williams no longer could hear it.

14

'Please wait in here for a moment. The doctor will be along in a minute or two.' The nurse ushered Theresa and Phil into Dr Richards' room and then departed.

They sat down in silence. They both felt strangely uneasy about seeing Gideon. What would they say to him about the fire, and about the death of his parents?

At last Theresa said in a very quiet voice, 'It will be awful breaking the news to him. He has already been told everything, apparently, but they can't tell if he has absorbed what they have told him.'

'I expect he does know,' Phil said, on reflection. 'Probably his mind just refuses to think about it. Deep inside himself he may understand. It will take time and patience to get him to come to terms with it, though.'

'Yes,' Theresa said. 'The trouble is I don't know how to approach him. I don't want to disturb him any more than is necessary. Sometimes I think that even seeing me will upset him and remind him of that awful night.'

'Perhaps if we take the lead from him . . .' Phil suggested. 'I think it's better to respond to whatever mood he's in than try to force too much on him.'

'I suppose you're right,' Theresa agreed. 'You can't plan how to deal with someone in the abstract. I guess we'll just know how to behave when we see him. If he's terribly quiet and won't speak I'll just sit with him. But it does worry me, not knowing what he's going to be like.'

Both of them sat quietly again, thinking of Gideon, trying to imagine what it would be like for a child of that age to lose both his parents.

But Phil felt uneasy for another reason as well, and he

couldn't speak to Theresa about it. Ever since he had known Theresa she had been protective about her brother. It was only after he had got really close to her that she was prepared to admit that there was something strange and unattractive about the boy. Since the accident – and it was only natural, he supposed – she had built up a picture of him, based on pity and affection, which did not correspond at all to Gideon's real personality. Theresa was a warm and generous person; all she could think of was that the boy had undergone a dreadful ordeal, and had probably suffered terribly as a result. She seemed to have forgotten completely what Gideon was really like.

Even Phil had at first been moved so much by pity that he had overlooked Gideon's sinister ways. But when they had gone back to the old house and seen the skeletons of Mrs MacKenzie's fish floating on the ornamental pond, it had brought back that unpleasant incident with terrible force. There was no doubt that Gideon *had* maliciously killed the fish. The greater horror of the fire the next day had made them forget that. Now, although he still felt sorry for Gideon, he could not help thinking of what the boy used to be like. His manner was distant and offensive and he stared at people in a most disconcerting way. Phil had always suspected that the boy was disturbed, and that had been confirmed by the fish incident. He didn't really like the thought of Gideon living with Theresa, but he felt there was nothing he could do about it. But perhaps Gideon would become a nicer person. He had always seemed to be entirely without warmth and emotion; perhaps his terrible experience would cure him of that, and make him more responsive and caring.

Phil stood up, suddenly feeling restless. 'I wonder where that doctor is. We've been here for at least fifteen minutes.' He looked at Theresa and saw that her eyes were filled with tears.

'Poor kid,' she muttered.

Phil went across to her. 'I know,' he said, and then he added, his eyes darkening, 'He's lucky to have you.'

'I wonder what's through that door?' Theresa said, attempting to brighten herself.

They both looked over at the far wall behind Dr Richards' desk. Just before the corner was a door, slightly open.

'Go and have a look,' he said.

She walked across the room to the far door.

'Well, is it a cloakroom?' Phil asked her with a laugh.

'No,' she said, 'it appears to be some sort of laboratory.' She went into the doorway of the adjoining room. 'Yes,' she called back to Phil. 'It's a laboratory.'

He followed her across the floor and looked into the room with her. Apart from a long low central table the room was empty. Round the walls were shelves, and over by the window stood a row of white sinks. The shelves were lined with rows of bottles which appeared to contain a variety of different chemicals. The place had a spartan, clinical atmosphere.

'Oh, there you are.'

They both turned, slightly embarrassed to be caught looking through the door, but Dr Richards was smiling and waved away their apologies. 'I'm sorry to keep you so long,' he said, closing the door to the little anteroom. He told them that it was his pharmacy, where he made up medicines for patients in the hospital.

Phil and Theresa went back to the two chairs before his desk and Dr Richards sat down facing them.

'We have been having a lot of trouble at Glendale this last week,' he told them. 'In fact, that is why I had to keep you waiting.' He looked at them with a grave face. 'The truth is we've had two tragedies here, one following closely upon the other.' He passed his hand across his brow. 'One of our nurses had a most horrible road accident. She ran out into a main road and was run over by a bus.' He shook his head silently. 'She was a most sensible and calm person. Someone must have been chasing her. It was so out of character . . .' His voice trailed away. 'I'm sorry,' he said. 'I shouldn't be troubling you with all this.'

Theresa reassured him. 'We're terribly sorry. It sounds an awful accident.'

Dr Richards smiled at her. 'Then, as I say, another very sad thing happened.' His voice lowered. 'A patient died here last night in the most appalling circumstances. I won't go into the details, but I felt I had to mention it to you. You see, we're a very close-knit community here. You can imagine how disturbing it is for the other patients. So you won't find us in our usual spirits, I'm afraid.' He cleared his throat. 'Which brings me to Gideon. The nurse who died was one who had been specially allocated to look after him. The news couldn't be kept back. These things spread quickly in an institution like this. I am afraid he may be severely affected. And Mr Williams, the patient who died, had been sharing a room with Gideon until only the night before. It is most unfortunate. It is quite likely that his recovery will be hampered by these two events.'

Phil and Theresa were distressed by what Dr Richards told them. 'I'm so sorry,' was all that they were able to say. They could see how upset he was and each felt like an intruder into his personal grief. 'We could come back another day,' Theresa offered. She desperately wanted to see Gideon but she guessed at all the extra problems posed for the staff by the two tragedies.

'Oh no,' the doctor told her. 'Thank you for suggesting it. But we must carry on as normal, you know. That is the only way to help the rest of the patients cope with what has happened. And I really feel that it might do Gideon a lot of good to see you.' His face clouded over. 'We still haven't managed to get him to speak, and, as I said, his case is a lot more difficult because of what has happened here. Originally, I had hopes of his making a fast recovery. In fact, he still seems quite well in all other respects.' He leaned forward to look at them. 'You know, the strange thing is he doesn't seem to be troubled by the two deaths here. He has shown no signs of grief, unlike the other patients. He still keeps very distant. He appears to be impervious.' He gave them a grave look. 'But of course this distancing of himself is a result of his disturbance. I've seen such cases of shock before. As I mentioned to you on the telephone, we have told him about the death of his parents. And I don't know how much he saw on the night of the fire at your house.' Dr Richards spoke in a soft voice, knowing that Theresa also had lost her parents. 'You must have suffered a lot yourself, as well,' he added sympathetically.

Theresa nodded. Her eyes were brimming with tears again. 'How terrible it must be for Gideon,' was all she could say. 'What a lot of tragic things . . .'

'Yes,' Dr Richards said, coming from behind his desk and putting his hand on Theresa's shoulder. 'So many things to bear at once. I know how hard it must be for him. We must all do what we can.'

'You're very kind,' Theresa said through her tears.

Phil was silent. His face was dark and heavy. The words of the doctor kept passing over and over again through his mind. He thought of the deaths of the nurse and the patient. At one level he felt immense pity for Gideon, and yet at another, he was gravely disturbed. Everything seemed to be centred around that boy. Without really knowing why, Phil had a sense of foreboding. He felt, though he could not explain it, that there was something sinister in all this, and that Gideon was at the core.

Later, when they walked down the long corridors to the day-room, the image of the floating fish skeletons fixed itself into his mind. He shivered, picturing the blanched white bones, as though they were some sign, some token of grizzly and agonising death to come. He closed his eyes, but the image remained. Stark white bones bobbing this way and that on the surface of the pond.

15

'There's Gideon,' Dr Richards said.

Theresa and Phil looked through the glass panel in the door of the day-room.

'He always sits by that window,' the doctor mused. 'Even if the weather is good he rarely goes into the garden. I would like him to go out more.'

They saw Gideon on the other side of the room. He was staring out through the window and had not noticed them yet. As they walked over to him Theresa felt a lump rise in her throat. He looked so small and forlorn sitting alone by the window. There was hardly anybody else in the room, for outside the sun was shining brightly, and most of the inmates were sitting on the lawn. Theresa could see them in a quiet and dismal row just beyond the open window.

At last Gideon became aware of their presence. He ignored Dr Richards and Phil but gave a small smile of welcome to his sister. She was relieved that he recognised her, for it had occurred to her from time to time that he would not.

The smile brought out the full force of her emotion and she rushed up to him and took him in her arms. 'Oh, Gideon,' she cried. 'I'm so glad to see you! I'm so glad!' She knelt on the floor before him and rocked him, forward and back, against her. Although he was not responsive he did not actively resist. So she held him there for minute after minute, unwilling to release him now that she had finally come to him. 'It seems so long,' she whispered. 'Such a long time. And tell me, dear, how are you? I hope you're not suffering too much.' At last she let him go, but even so she sat very close to his chair, as though she was afraid she might lose him.

Dr Richards and Phil hung back slightly, allowing Theresa her moment of intimacy with her brother, but now she was sitting on the floor and Gideon leant back in his chair, Phil went forward to join them. 'Hello, Gideon,' he said to the boy, but, as he had expected, there was no reply.

Dr Richards patted the boy on the head and looked at Phil as if to say, 'I'm afraid it really is impossible to get him to say anything.'

'There you are,' he said to Gideon. 'I told you your sister was coming to see you.'

'Gideon,' Theresa said. 'Are you pleased to see me? I wish you could say something. I do wish you would speak to us.'

'I will speak to *you*,' Gideon said quite calmly. 'But I don't wish to speak to anyone else.'

The three of them stared at him in amazement.

'Gideon! You spoke! You spoke to me,' Theresa said happily, not caring about what he had said, only glad that he had said *something*. She smiled at him. 'Oh, and I was afraid that you couldn't speak. But you can, you can!'

'Of course I can speak,' Gideon replied in a collected voice. 'Who told you that I wasn't able to?'

'Well,' she began, looking at Dr Richards. 'Well, you haven't been talking, have you?'

'No,' he said. 'But then I haven't wanted to.' As he spoke, Gideon looked away from them and stared once more through the window. There was a feeling of cold disinterest about him.

'You are a very naughty boy, then,' Theresa said incongruously, as though addressing a lovable child. 'Everyone has been very worried about you.'

Gideon turned back to Theresa. He wished she wouldn't talk so foolishly, wished she would not refer to him as a 'naughty boy', especially in front of the other two. He glanced over at Dr Richards and Phil. Dr Richards gave him an indulgent smile but Phil looked tight and withdrawn. 'When can we go home?' Gideon asked his sister. 'When are you going to take me away?'

'As soon as I can,' Theresa said earnestly.

While Gideon was having this conversation with his sister, Dr Richards was standing quietly in a state of some amazement. He was quite unable to believe that Gideon had spoken at last, and apparently with no difficulty at all. He didn't attempt to say anything himself, not wanting to drive the boy into another silence. It was better, he reasoned, for Gideon to speak to his sister than to not speak at all. He hoped that if he was patient for a few more minutes the boy would talk to him too. But when, finally, he said to Gideon, 'Are you feeling better now that Theresa has come to see you?' he received nothing but a cold stare.

'Answer the doctor,' Theresa said to her brother, but Dr Richards indicated to her by a wave of the hand that it would be wrong to try to force him.

Then, ignoring the doctor altogether, Gideon merely repeated his question. 'When are you going to take me home?'

Theresa looked at Dr Richards for guidance, not knowing what to say. She wanted to take Gideon away immediately, but she wasn't certain if this was possible.

'Well,' Dr Richards said. 'You seem to be coming along nicely. I should think it might be all right in a day or two.'

'I want to go now,' Gideon insisted, directing himself

solely to Theresa. 'You must take me.'

'It's not up to her, is it?' Phil was unable to keep an edge of dislike out of his voice. Really, even if the boy had been through a lot, he was intolerable.

Gideon was silent for a moment as though he was considering something.

'We all want the best for you,' Dr Richards said in an amiable voice. 'And really, I would prefer to have you here with us for a few more days. So we can keep an eye on you,' he added with a wink.

Gideon stared at Dr Richards, irritated by the friendly manner and the wink. Why did he have to interfere? 'There's nothing the matter with me,' he said to Theresa. 'Don't you believe me? I'm speaking, aren't I? Well what's wrong, then? You thought I couldn't speak, but now you know I can. I just don't want to talk to *them*. Is that any reason to keep me here?'

Phil's face reddened. He resented the boy's attitude.

'Now then, Gideon,' Dr Richards said. 'There's no need to get upset. You'll be home before very long. There's nothing to worry about. Now, wouldn't you like to go into the garden with your sister? It's a beautiful day.' While he was speaking he noted the antagonism on Gideon's face. *Yes*, he thought. *We ought to hang on to him for a while longer. He's quite obviously still very disturbed by his recent experiences*. Secretly he was concerned, but there was no evidence of this in his face. 'It's the hottest day we've had,' he said.

'Yes,' Theresa said. 'Let's go into the gardens. They look lovely. You can show me round,' she told Gideon.

'Oh, very well. But there's nothing to look at. It's very boring out there.'

'Gideon,' Theresa said. 'Don't say things like that.'

Dr Richards laughed. 'Oh, don't worry about what he says as long as he says something. That's all I care about.'

Theresa spent the next hour with Gideon, while Phil,

deeply perturbed, walked by himself on the lawn or chatted lightly to the other inmates who were sitting in a row in front of the windows of the day-room. It was obvious that Gideon didn't want him to be present, and really, if he had thought about it beforehand, he would have guessed the boy would behave in this way. He had never known Gideon to be pleasant or polite.

At tea-time Theresa and Phil left the hospital. Gideon was sullen, but seemed to accept that he could not leave that afternoon. He made no further fuss, only adding that he would like to go as soon as possible.

'Of course you shall,' Theresa told him. 'I'm sure they won't keep you long. I'll speak to the doctor.'

Gideon waved to them from the window of the day-room as they went away down the drive.

'You see,' Theresa said to Phil. 'He really has recovered.'

Phil nodded gloomily. 'Because you heard him speaking, you mean?' he said.

'Well, yes. And he doesn't seem to be troubled by anything.'

'And do you think that is natural?' Phil asked her.

'What do you mean?' Theresa was hurt that Phil was so critical of Gideon.

'Do you think his behaviour is natural?' Phil kicked at a loose stone on the driveway. He knew he was upsetting her, but he was tired of the silence which had grown up between them on the subject of Gideon. Now he had begun he would not stop. There was more to say, much more. 'Does he seem like a boy who has recently lost both his parents? Well, does he?'

'Phil! How could you say such a thing? It's a terrible thing to say. You're saying he doesn't care. You are actually telling me that Gideon doesn't care about the death of his parents!'

'Yes,' he said quietly. 'And there's something else,

something even worse.' He hesitated, for he didn't know quite how to begin. Then he said, 'Two people who were involved with Gideon in the hospital have died. Don't you think that is strange?' He was quiet then, unable to continue, then at last he went on, 'The policeman who found Gideon on the night of the fire had an accident. He also died. I heard about it. You didn't know that, did you? That's three people, Theresa.' He couldn't bring himself to say 'five', though that was in his thoughts.

Theresa stood still on the path. 'You are making the most terrible accusations. You are implying that Gideon had something to do with all those deaths.' She burst into a flood of angry tears. 'How dare you say things like that! I won't listen to you any more.' Then, without saying another word, she ran down the drive, ahead of him, not wanting to be with him.

'Theresa,' he called, but she did not stop. 'What about the fish?' He ran after her down the long driveway. 'Don't you remember what he did to the goldfish?'

'Stop it,' she screamed. 'I don't want to hear you.'

Gideon was still standing by the window, although they had long passed out of sight. There was a look of satisfaction on his face, and yet he was also troubled. He hated Phil. He hated him. That man was trying to turn Theresa against him. 'Don't listen to him,' he said to himself. 'Don't listen.' And, as if he could hear the bitter words between them, he put his hands over his ears.

Theresa and Phil were struggling together on the path. He was trying to hold her, trying to make her listen, and she was doing everything she could to get away from him.

'You saw the fish,' he shouted.

'Stop it! Stop it! Don't say any more!' Finally she tore herself away from him and ran out through the gates and along the road.

Phil hung back. If she didn't want to be with him, well, let her go. But his heart was heavy. He hadn't wanted to hurt her, and yet, he *had* wanted to make her see that something was wrong. He sensed that Gideon had something to do with the deaths that were constantly occurring, but at the same time he knew that it was crazy. He had wanted Theresa to listen to him, he had needed to talk to her, but at the same time he knew he had said the wrong things. What was he to do? He walked on slowly and fretfully towards the gates at the end of the drive.

Gideon turned back from the window. His eyes were gleaming. He went over to the nurse on duty and took a glass of orange juice from the tray, then he went back to his seat and began to sip at the cold orange liquid. 'I'll show them,' he thought. 'I'll show them all.'

16

Phil was in low spirits. After Theresa had left him outside Glendale he went into town. He resisted the temptation to go back to her flat, and, still feeling restless, was unwilling to go home. He spent several hours wandering about the streets, and from time to time went into one of the pubs, where he sat solitary and morose in a corner, not speaking to anyone. He was trying to sort things out in his mind, trying to assess exactly what it was that troubled him about Gideon. Although he had a suspicion that the boy was involved in the series of deaths which had recently taken place, he could not really see how Gideon could be blamed. He certainly could not have been present when the nurse died, and when the policeman met with his fatal accident Gideon was inside the station with a doctor, and not in the garage where the accident occurred. Phil had been to the police station and talked to the officer in charge. It was baffling.

Now it was getting on for eleven o'clock and he was still no nearer to a solution. He switched constantly from believing that the boy was guilty in some way, to feeling that he himself was deluded. He even felt ashamed, at times, of thinking that Gideon had started the fire which killed his parents. But though there seemed to be no case against Gideon, Phill still could not help a dark nagging doubt creeping into his mind. In his despair he drank more than he meant to and by the time he decided to go home his head was quite hazy and confused.

It was a sweetly scented warm June night, and he thought of going to see Theresa. He wanted to go to her, wanted to be with her, but he could not. How could he confront her with his deep and unspecified fears about her brother? What could he say? There seemed to be no foundation for his suspicions. Suspecting Gideon was a matter of instinct, nothing more, but he could not give it up. Theresa did not understand how he felt, and really he did not blame her. So he was dark and miserable as he walked to the railway station. His mind was filled with the thought of Theresa and himself and how Gideon seemed to be coming between them like a shadow which he could not wipe away. It was then, as he walked, that he began to visualise his own secret fear. The fear of rats.

Since childhood, whenever he had been ill or weak, he had imagined rats surrounding him and attacking him in the darkness. Once, when he had been in bed suffering from a childhood illness, rats had seemed to fill the room and climb up over the bed, tearing at the bedclothes and gnawing at his flesh. He had been in a high fever and sometimes the world had seemed vast and bearing down upon him. Sometimes it had seemed a minute thing and he had felt like some immense giant by contrast. But whichever way he had pictured the world inside his throbbing head, the rats had come. When the world was large the rats were huge king-sized creatures with terrible claws and great cavernous mouths, and when the world was small they had become tiny as pinpricks, but there had been thousands of them. And like pins they had jabbed into him. The horror of those small piercing teeth! He had screamed, but still they had come, and now, though he was no longer a child, something of the scream and the memory remained inside him.

At first he heard a sound of scuffling and saw red eyes watching him from the gardens of houses which he passed. He bit his teeth together, steeling himself against this old, familiar horror. He blinked his eyes, and the little glinting points of red vanished. His heartbeat was quieter. But they came again.

This time when they came they were closer, and there were more of them. Though he blinked his eyes to try and dispel the sight of them, they would not leave him. He held himself tight, sensing that if he weakened or faltered they would be upon him and he would feel the points of their sharp, bone-like little teeth. He could hear a noise too, which disturbed him more than the sight of the eyes. It was the sound of scurrying feet. The faster he walked the faster the sound of the feet became. And he could hear paper being ripped and shredded. Once, a torn-off sheet of newspaper flapped against his leg as he walked. The sight of the paper – because of its association with the ripping teeth of the rats – drove him into a near frenzy. It was then that he began to run. He knew it was foolish to run and he knew it was unnecessary. The rats were not really all around him, he was only imagining that they were, and so he did not need to escape them. But he could not help it. And the longer he ran the more he terrified himself, the more he believed that he was running away from something that had real existence. He could hear them scampering behind him. Sometimes there was a scrambling noise on the walls of the gardens to his left.

More were coming. From each garden others came to join those who were already in pursuit of him. He heard their feet as they leapt from the garden walls.

He was near the centre of the town and he felt safer. He had not actually seen the bodies of the rats, only the glint of their eyes in the dark, and heard the horrible scuffling feet. If he could get into the centre, where it was light, he felt that he would have the strength to resist them. He must not give in, he must force himself to overcome their power. For he was still aware that they were in his mind only and had no substance. 'I must fight,' he thought, as he ran.

Once, he fancied he saw the face of Gideon. The boy was standing just ahead of him. It reminded him of the time he had seen Gideon in the garden of the old house. Quietly watching, still as the trees. He and Theresa had looked through a window and there the boy had been. Sinister. Standing on the lawn looking at nothing in particular. There had been something menacing about him. Now Phil could see him as on that day, with the same vacant expression and the same uncanny intent. He forced himself to think instead of Theresa with her smiling face. Fighting off the sight of the boy, he concentrated his mind on Theresa. Somehow the sight of her face seemed to erase the sight of Gideon's. Even the sound of the rats grew more distant as he thought of her.

When he reached the town centre he had a moment's peace. There was no sign of the sharp, blood-red eyes, and the scampering noise had gone. He stopped running. What a fool he had been. What a damned fool. How could he have reacted in that way? His breath became quieter, he began to relax. But that was his undoing. In the very act of relaxing he lost his power to resist. He became soft and penetrable, ripe for the teeth of rats. At once he realised it, but it was too late. As he was standing by the edge of the road he saw three or four of them racing towards him. Fur sleek as oil, grey, almost black. Feet pink. Flesh pink with the suggestion of blood. A look of death about them. A contaminating look, as though they fed on putrefied waste, mingled with disease. Decaying flesh, fetid stagnant blood, the great stinking sewers below the earth: a knowledge of all this filth shone in the eyes of the rats.

He screamed. The street was deserted and no one heard him. And, as though they heard the scream and knew his weakness, they came faster. Sleek grey-black fur. Pink feet. He was almost sick.

He must get to the station. He bit his teeth hard against one another, trying to gather up his strength. He must fight his weakness, must resist them. He knew he was hallucinating. Thank God, he knew that. They were so vivid he was nearly convinced they were really there. He forced himself to remember that they were only in his mind. If he lost sight of that he could not survive.

At last he was at the station, but at this time of night it was dim and bleak and deserted. He ran the length of the platform, hoping that someone would be there. If there was just one person, he would be able to talk to him. The fears would dissipate. But there was no one, not a soul. It was so disheartening. 'O God, let there be somebody,' he called out. No one. Not another passenger, not even a porter or a ticket collector. He looked into the waiting-room, but that too was empty. The platform stretched out, lit by the dingy yellow lights that seemed to struggle against the encroaching darkness. He had no spirit left to fight. He slumped down against a bench on the long, straight platform.

That was when he saw them. They were scampering along the platform. They were climbing up from the track, over the concrete edge, coming from the shadow into the light. Coming towards him. It was no dream now. He could smell them and hear them and see them.

For an instant Gideon's face appeared before him. A mocking face. The round, wide eyes had narrowed into two slits. Then that image faded and there were only the rats.

They were upon him. He felt their needle teeth pass through his clothes and enter his flesh. He was too horrified to scream. His breathing was slow and heavy, and with every breath he could smell them, the acrid stench of them. It overpowered him. And there were so many of them. Little shrill squeaking noises which drove him insane accompanied every move. They scurried away and then darted back to his body, claiming it like some piece of deserted meat. They burrowed into the soft flesh of his cheek, and all the time he was thinking, 'My eyes! They will tear my eyes out and dig into the raw red cavities behind.' He moaned to himself as he lay there.

But there was another sound that he heard above their rapacious squealing. The train was coming. He could feel the reverberation of its approach through the concrete beneath his body. He dragged himself to the edge of the platform. Any escape, anything was better than this. He thought of Theresa and, strangely, for a moment his awareness of the rats retreated. The pain lessened. But he was falling. There was nothing to hold on to. He was falling on to the track. In one terrified moment he realised that he was going down right into the path of the oncoming train. He saw the bulk of the engine looming out of the darkness. The bright yellow lights, the mighty crescendo of sound. '*Theresa*,' he screamed, and her face in his mind was his last conscious thought.

17

When Theresa got home she sat down on a chair and stared at the wall opposite. She felt terrible. Her head was aching and heavy, and her eyes smarting. But there were no tears. It was as if she had no tears left. She kept thinking of what Phil had said, of what he had implied. He had suggested that somehow, Gideon . . .

No! At first, she pushed the implications of Phil's words out of her mind. It was impossible, it couldn't be true. How could he say such things about Gideon? She would not think of it. She saw only the patterns of the paper on the wall, yellow scrolls twisting around each other. She focused her eyes on the regular lines. But though she concentrated on the pattern, tried to lose herself in the bright colour, gradually the memory of her row with Phil came back. It kept insinuating itself in her mind. And she could hear his last words, the ones he had called out as she had run away. 'The goldfish.'

In the yellow patterns on the wall the shape of the fish appeared, then broke up, dissipated, and became only twists of yellow on paper again. As she moved her head from side to side the rhythm of the tiny bodies on the still water, barely moving, re-established itself. The paper before her appeared to undulate. She had fled from Phil because of what he had said. It couldn't be true. But still, unwillingly, the thought of the white bones that they had seen, the stripped skeletons, came back to her. In front of her eyes the lines of the paper took on the appearance of the neat, needle-like bones. And into her mind came the memory of the afternoon before the fire. The images of faces rose and drifted past her. Mrs MacKenzie, standing by the pool. Her mouth was closed tight and there were tears in her eyes. Then she had opened her mouth and said, 'He ought to be put away.' Theresa thought of her own mother. She could see her lips turned up, a look of disgust on her face. She had stared at Gideon as if he was a stranger. Her father had stood in quiet shock, and then he had become angry, terribly angry. And Gideon – cold eyes, supremely self-contained – staring at them. Then her father had slapped him and . . .

'I won't think about it,' she said out loud. She screwed up her eyes into two tight hard knots. Gideon was only a boy.

She got up from the chair and went into the kitchen, but the thought of food made her feel sick. She couldn't eat anything. She turned on the tap and drank a glass of water. It was cool, refreshing. She dipped her finger into the running water and touched her forehead with the cold drops. 'I must look after Gideon,' she told herself. 'He hasn't got anyone else.' But there was something empty and hollow in her words. She was trying to override the insistent doubts that she could feel deep inside herself. 'It's irrational,' she thought. 'How could he . . .?' She turned off the tap and switched on the radio, hoping that the sound would obliterate her unpleasant thoughts. 'Damn Phil,' she said to herself.

The late afternoon drifted into evening. Theresa wandered from room to room in the flat, trying to escape from her thoughts. 'Damn Phil,' she thought again. Incidents from the past kept coming into her mind, but she refused to put them together, to make a pattern, to draw conclusions. Something about Gideon at school, just before they moved. The evenings he had spent in the cellar. The strange way he had of looking at people.

No, it all meant nothing, and she hated herself for the little doubts which kept creeping into her mind.

Glancing at the clock, she saw that it was almost ten. She was so tired. She realised that in a way she had been sitting up waiting for Phil to come, but now she sensed that he wasn't going to. 'I'll have an early night,' she thought.

On the way to her bedroom she looked into the small room that she had prepared for Gideon. All his things had been destroyed in the fire, so she had brought a few books and stuck posters on the wall, and tried to give the room a feeling of belonging to someone. But now, as she stood and looked around, she knew that it was not Gideon that she had prepared this room for. She had painted and decorated and bought things for some imaginary brother that she had never had. A boy who was mischievous and sometimes naughty, who could be irritating, even tiresome, and yet at the same time lovable, responsive, fun to be with. She sighed and closed the door. Well, it wasn't any good thinking of how Gideon might have been. He was what he was. But what was he?

She wished now that Phil had come round. The time seemed to drag without him. Sitting down on the side of her bed she had a sudden twinge of misgiving. Had she been too hard on Phil? She had been hurt by what he had said, but to run off like that . . . She could have stayed, they could have talked about it. What good had it done to leave him? Now they were both miserable. Closing her eyes she thought of Phil's face, but though she tried to concentrate, his features eluded her. A dark cloud kept obscuring his face so that she could not see him properly.

At last, feeling disconsolate, she got into bed and pulled up the covers around her. Although it was a warm summer night she felt slightly cold and a little shiver passed over her body. She closed her eyes and sleep came fast. But it was a troubled sleep that she fell into. She twisted around in the bed feeling first cold, then hot, then cold again. There seemed to be no peace. She dreamed of

Gideon. He was standing in a garden. At first, she thought it was the green lawn at Glendale, but when she looked closely she saw that it was the garden of the old house. For a long time he stood there, not moving. Then he turned. He was looking at someone. With a start she realised that he was looking at Phil. Phil was standing by the pond. Then he went over to Gideon. They were arguing. She couldn't hear any of the words, but she could see from their faces that they were angry.

As she tossed and turned in the bed the dream became fragmented. The old house became confused with Glendale. Her mother and father were sitting in two chairs in the room where they had visited Gideon. Somewhere she could hear someone screaming. She turned round to see who it was, but everything was dark. There was nothing there. She was alone in the darkness. Far off she could see a round pool of dim yellow light, and in that light there was someone slumped down.

'Get up,' Theresa called out in her sleep. 'Don't just lie there. Get up.' She could hear the sound of Gideon's laughter, then she heard his voice.

You must take me away from here. You'll look after me, won't you, Theresa?

Then, suddenly, there was a riveting scream. It tore through her ears and through her head. Gideon was standing in the little room which she had prepared for him, looking strangely out of place. Theresa began to shake him. 'What have you done, Gideon?' she said. 'Tell me what you've done. Tell me!' She was angry with him. She was going to slap his face, when she realised that he wasn't there after all. She was alone again. But still, echoing through her ears, was that terrible scream.

Immediately she was awake. She sat up in bed and turned on the light. It took her a while to remember where she was. At first, she thought she was in her bedroom at the old house. Then she remembered. The images of the dream came back to her with frightening clarity. She got up out of bed and went back to the sitting-room. It was one o'clock. It was late, but even so, she had to ring Phil. She *must* speak to him. For some reason her mind was in a turmoil of fear. As she dialled the number her heart beat wildly inside her. There was no answer for a long time, then she heard his father's sleepy voice.

'No,' he said, in answer to Theresa's question. 'He hasn't come back. We thought he was staying with you.'

Her body ran cold. Where could he be? She knew that something was wrong, and in another minute she had put her coat on as though she meant to go and look for him. It was then that the doorbell rang, and when she saw the policeman standing in the doorway her heart nearly broke. She put out a hand to steady herself.

'There's been an accident,' the policeman said.

18

Theresa came through the doors of the ward and when she saw Phil in the end bed she could not stop herself from calling out. 'Phil.'

The patients and other visitors turned round to look at her, but she did not notice them. She ran down the ward and threw herself on to the chair beside his bed. It was obvious that she wanted to throw her arms around him but was holding herself back in case she hurt him.

'Come on,' he said softly. 'I'm not so fragile.'

For a long time they simply held each other. The tears ran down her face. Lines of strain had etched themselves around her eyes.

'The police came round to the flat,' she told him. 'I was

so shocked to hear what happened. Then the doctors wouldn't let me see you. Three days I had to wait! You can't believe what I went through.' The sobs broke into her words. 'I even thought that you might die.'

Phil squeezed her shoulder, not knowing how to comfort her properly, what to say.

'I couldn't stand it,' Theresa continued. 'Losing you, after everything else.'

There was another long pause. They just held each other closely and Theresa's crying gradually subsided.

'I'm going to be all right,' Phil said gently.

Theresa pulled back and looked at him. 'Your poor face,' she said, raising her hand and touching the bandages on his head. 'How on earth did it happen?'

'I don't know,' Phil said. 'I'm not sure.'

'You tripped and fell over the edge of the platform.' Her face coloured slightly. 'The policeman said you had been drinking.'

Phil nodded grimly. 'I had had a few drinks,' he said. 'But I wasn't really drunk, you know.'

'So what did happen? How could you trip just like that?'

'Have you been to see Gideon?' Phil asked, avoiding her question.

'Yes,' Theresa said, watching Phil closely. 'I have been to see him. He's still at Glendale. They want to keep him there under observation for a few more days. Dr Richards isn't exactly happy with him. He still won't speak to anyone except me.'

'Don't have him to live with you,' Phil blurted out. 'You mustn't. It's . . . dangerous.'

'Oh Phil,' Theresa said. 'How can I let him down? Where would he go?' She paused. 'I've been thinking over what you said the other day about Gideon. There *is* something strange about him, I know. But in the past you've always been the one to say he'd be all right. He's not dangerous.'

'You've always been so protective about him,' Phil said. 'I understand that. But now, I can't help saying to you that I think he *is* dangerous.' His voice lowered. 'There is no proof, but I think that he started the fire.'

Theresa gave a little start. 'He couldn't have,' she said.

Phil looked at Theresa seriously. 'I know what I'm saying is very upsetting to you, but it's important. I'd never forgive myself if anything happened to *you*.'

Theresa held his hand. 'But the other day,' she said, 'you talked about the policeman, and the nurse, and that other patient at Glendale. Gideon couldn't have had anything to do with their deaths.'

'I'll come to that in a minute,' Phil said. 'But first, I want to talk about the fire.'

She nodded, dreading what Phil would say and yet knowing that she must listen.

'You told me that Gideon was the first one out of the house. Mrs MacKenzie saw him when she was coming down her stairs.'

'Yes, but that doesn't mean anything,' Theresa said.

'Did he come and knock at your door before he left the house?'

'No,' Theresa admitted. 'At least, I didn't hear him.'

'So he left the house without trying to warn you,' Phil said. 'Just walked out by himself.'

'You're making too much of it,' Theresa said. 'He didn't just walk out, he ran out. He was frightened. That was quite natural. He's only twelve years old. Just a boy.'

'And he didn't try to rouse your mum and dad, didn't try and get help?'

'The house was blazing, Phil. You can't imagine what it was like!' She frowned. 'And anyway, if he'd started the fire the police would have found evidence.'

Phil nodded glumly. 'I said there was no proof.' His voice was flat.

Theresa's face paled. She leant forward in a confidential manner. 'I have also thought he might have started it. Since your accident I have gone over and over it. But I can't believe it. And as for the deaths of those other people, it's even more incredible to suggest that Gideon was responsible. It seems unfair that just because he's strange you should think these evil things of him.'

For a moment or two there was a silence again, then falteringly and quietly, Phil told her what had happened to *him*.

'I wasn't drunk,' he said. 'Something was moving my mind, making me think things and do things that I wouldn't normally do. I felt as if I was being controlled.' He told her about the rats. He looked straight at Theresa. 'But there came a time when it didn't seem like imagination. They had become real. I could smell them, Theresa.' He was shaking now and he gave a little groan.

Theresa winced. 'Phil,' she said softly. 'It's all right now.'

'I wasn't hallucinating,' Phil said. 'It wasn't like that. Somehow, I can't explain it, something had got inside my head, making me think these things, making me see them.'

Theresa said quietly. 'And you think it was Gideon.'

Phil sighed. 'It sounds crazy,' he said. 'To hear the words out loud sounds crazy.'

'But that's what you think,' Theresa insisted.

'Yes,' Phil admitted. There was a pause then he said, 'Do you remember what they said about that nurse?'

'She was run over.'

'Yes,' Phil said. 'But they said it was as if she was running away from something. They didn't know what that something was, and they never found out. She was so frightened that she just ran out blindly into the road, ran under the bus. Do you know what I think she was running away from?'

Theresa shook her head mutely.

'She was running away from something terrible, so terrible that the fear in her completely took over. She didn't know where she was going or what she did. I think she was running away from her own worst fear.'

Theresa was shaking and her face was white.

Phil went on. 'The patient who died in the hospital. Did you know he had a persecution complex?'

'No,' Theresa said. She could hardly speak. Her tongue was dry inside her mouth.

'I talked to one of the nurses when you were with Gideon,' Phil told her. 'They all thought he was getting better. And perhaps he was until . . . until Gideon came along.' Phil smiled grimly, there was no humour in his face. 'On the night he killed himself he was heard screaming that everyone was after him. He killed himself to get away from them.'

Theresa lifted up her hands to her ears. 'I'm sorry, Phil,' she said. 'I can't hear any more. It can't be true. It doesn't make sense. It's madness.'

'Don't let him come and live with you,' Phil whispered. 'Please. For me.'

'I don't know what to think,' Theresa said. 'It . . . it's just too . . .'

Phil's voice was low. 'There are things that happen . . .things in this world . . . things beyond our understanding. It is possible that some people have special powers.'

Theresa shook her head. 'How can it be?' she said.

And Phil didn't have the answer.

19

'Come in, Gideon,' Dr Richards said.

A nurse was standing just behind Gideon in the doorway. 'Do you want me to stay, doctor?' she asked.

'No, that will be all right. You can leave us together.' Dr Richards was determined to do everything he could to get Gideon to speak. He had to see a sign of improvement before he could let the boy go, and also, there were a few questions he wanted to ask him.

Gideon came in and sat on the chair before the desk.

Dr Richards smiled at him and offered him a sweet from the tin which he always kept for the younger patients. 'Now I know you can speak,' he said, as Gideon unwrapped the sweet which he had given him. 'And so I know you can understand what I'm saying. You want to go home as soon as possible, don't you?' There was no reply and so he said, 'Of course you do.'

Gideon sat and stared at him. His eyes did not flicker. He didn't like this man, didn't like him at all, and he resented the fact that Dr Richards had power over him.

'I haven't applied any pressure to you, I know you've been through a great shock. But we've all been very worried about you. You must understand that, and realise that whatever we do is for your own good.' Dr Richards paused, feeling a certain spreading heat under his collar. There was something in the way the boy's hooded eyes stared unblinkingly that irritated and disturbed him. 'You have to understand,' he went on quickly, 'that I'm responsible for you. And it's very hard for me to allow you to leave here when you refuse to speak. You see, in refusing to speak you are showing us that there is something wrong with you.' He paused again and ran his finger round the collar of his shirt. 'Do you follow me?' he said.

Still Gideon stared at him unflinchingly.

'What I'm saying,' Dr Richards continued, his voice sounding a little more angry than he wanted it to, 'what I'm saying is that you really must start talking to me, answering my questions and telling me how you feel, before I can sign your release.' He smiled at Gideon. 'I don't want to keep you here any more than you want to be here.'

For a long time there was silence in the room. Dr Richards waited for his words to have effect.

Gideon stared at the doctor's face and then lowered his eyes and looked at the sweet in his hand. He'd have to speak to this man or they'd never let him go. After a few minutes had gone by he nodded slowly. 'All right,' he said. 'I'll answer your questions. I'll talk to you if you want me to.'

Dr Richards breathed a sigh of relief, but somehow he felt that getting Gideon to speak was an unsatisfactory kind of achievement. He hadn't really broken through to the lad, Gideon had just submitted in order to get his own way. But at least it was a first step. Perhaps all the rest would come later. 'That's better,' he said, trying to put more confidence in his voice than he felt. He picked up a pencil. 'Now let's start with a few questions,' he said. 'Over the last few weeks we've told you, even though you haven't been speaking, about the things that have happened.' He coughed. 'About the fire, I mean. Do you remember those things we told you?'

'Do you mean about my parents dying?' Gideon asked, putting the sweet into his mouth. His voice was matter of fact.

Dr Richards looked at him sharply. The boy seemed so cool about it. He made a little note on the paper before him. 'Yes,' he said. The boy obviously had a block, wasn't allowing his true feelings to surface. Mmm, that was a difficulty.

'Well, what do you want to know?' Gideon asked him.

For a moment Dr Richards was nonplussed. He was used to dealing with patients, but he couldn't decide how to handle Gideon. He feared it was all going to take longer than he had thought. He had expected any conversation about the fire to be a delicate process. Usually he knew exactly how to proceed on such occasions. But Gideon was so extremely prosaic that it quite threw him. He had assumed the boy was repressing his true feelings, and really that must be the case. On the other hand . . .was it possible he was really this callous? 'Tell me what you remember about the fire,' he said.

'There's nothing to tell,' Gideon said. 'There was a fire.'

'Well, what was the fire like?' Dr Richards wanted to tap the root of his experience.

Gideon shrugged. 'Yellow flames,' he said.

'And smoke, was there a lot of smoke?'

'Of course,' Gideon replied.

Dr Richards ran his tongue along his upper lip. 'And your mum and dad?' Normally he wouldn't have said this, not at this stage, but Gideon was so unresponsive, so unemotional. He had to draw his feelings out of him.

'They were trapped in their room and they died,' Gideon said.

'I see.' Dr Richards wrote something on the paper.

Gideon's eyes narrowed. What was he writing? 'Will I be able to go home with Theresa now?' he asked.

Dr Richards looked at him uneasily. 'In a little while,' he said.

'Why not now?' Gideon's voice was sharp, penetrating. 'Why can't I go now?'

'Well,' Dr Richards began. 'We really want to make

sure that you are quite . . . well.'

'You said if I spoke then I could go. Now you won't let me. You lied to me.'

'Now, Gideon,' Dr Richards said. 'I'm not saying that you can't go home.' He paused.

'I want to go home today,' Gideon said.

Dr Richards became firm. 'I know you've begun to speak,' he said. 'And that really does make a difference. Over the next few days we'll see each other every afternoon for a little talk. I think it would be helpful to you. You've had a terrible shock, and it's not easy getting over a shock like that.' While he was speaking, Dr Richards had been looking down at the file before him. Now he looked up at Gideon's face. Gideon was staring at him again. 'Gideon?' he said. The boy's eyelids flickered. In that moment the boy seemed sinister to the doctor. He felt a wave of heat rush up under his collar. There was something wrong with the boy, something very wrong. His responses were totally abnormal. He dragged his eyes away from the boy's face, shook his head to clear it, and made another note on the file. 'I think that will be all for this afternoon. I'll see you later on in the day-room. And I'll get the nurse to bring you up here to my office tomorrow at the same time.'

Gideon stood up.

'Oh, there was something else,' Dr Richards said in a casual voice, as if he had just had an afterthought. But the question he was about to ask had been carefully planned. 'Sit down a minute, would you?'

Gideon sat down and the doctor watched his face closely.

'Nurse Gower, she was on duty the other night, says that just before Mr Williams . . . that you went to the bathroom. Is that so?'

The room went very quiet. Gideon did not answer. He kept his face clear but inside he was very angry at the question.

'Did you go to the bathroom?' Dr Richards asked sharply.

'Yes,' Gideon said.

'And on your way there, did you stop and talk to Mr Williams, or did he talk to you?'

'No,' Gideon said.

'He was often talking to you, Mr Williams, wasn't he,' Dr Richards said. 'I often saw him talking to you. Are you sure he didn't say anything that night? Are you sure you didn't say anything to him?'

'Of course I'm sure,' Gideon said.

Dr Richards nodded. 'All right, Gideon,' he said. 'You can go now.' The boy was lying. He knew that, could see it quite clearly. The unexpected question had made him reveal himself, as Dr Richards had hoped it would. 'All right, Gideon,' he repeated. 'You may leave now. I'll see you later.'

Gideon stood up and walked to the door. Why was the doctor asking these questions? Why couldn't they just leave him alone? Why didn't they let him go home? He hated Dr Richards. Poking around with questions.

When Gideon was gone Dr Richards sat at the desk in some consternation. What had the boy said to Williams? He was convinced that he had upset him in some way. He was determined to get the truth out of him, but he knew it wouldn't be easy.

20

Theresa sat in the headmaster's study, her face set in hard determination. She didn't know exactly why she had come, didn't know what she would find out, or whether she would find out anything at all. But, even so, she felt quite determined. She must find out whatever there was to know about Gideon. Phil was convinced that Gideon had had something to do with his accident, and she would do everything she could to find out the truth. When she had left Phil at the hospital, she had decided straight away that she would come back to Gideon's old school and question them about what had happened and why they had forced him to leave the school.

'Good afternoon,' Mr Franks said, coming into the room.

'Oh, good afternoon,' Theresa said. She knew Mr Franks, for she herself had attended the same school when she was a child.

'It's Theresa Tanner, isn't it,' he said, and she could tell by the slight frown on his face that it was the incident with Gideon that he remembered rather than her.

'Yes,' she said. 'Thank you for letting me come to see you. There are a few questions I'd like to ask you, as I said on the telephone.'

'Ah,' Mr Franks said, taking a chair opposite Theresa. 'Well, I hope I will be able to help you.'

Theresa came straight to the point. 'It's about my brother, Gideon,' she said.

Mr Franks' eyes clouded. 'Oh, Gideon,' he said. 'Yes, I somehow thought that what you wanted to say would have something to do with him.'

Theresa explained to the headmaster all that had happened. She told him about the accident, and said that Gideon was causing her great concern because he wasn't behaving normally and wasn't speaking. She said that she thought it was important for her to know as much as she could about Gideon in order for her to be able to help him. She knew that some incident had happened at the school but she didn't know what. 'And that's what I've come here for,' she finished. 'Because I'd like you to tell me.'

'I'm sorry to hear about your parents,' Mr Franks said. 'I told your father all about it, of course, and I can understand why he never talked of it.'

Theresa frowned. 'What happened?' she asked urgently.

'Come along with me,' Mr Franks said. 'I want to take you to the biology room.' He led her through the school, trying to make polite conversation. But she could tell that he was upset by the memory of what had happened.

'Here we are,' he said, opening the door of the biology room. 'Ah, we're lucky, there's not a class in here at the moment.' On the benches around the room were cages of animals. Rabbits and rats, gerbils and hamsters. 'These are really pets,' he told her. 'You probably remember them yourself when you were in the younger classes.'

Theresa nodded. 'Yes,' she said with a smile. 'I looked after a rabbit one term.' She looked at Mr Franks, wondering what he was going to say.

'Out of school hours this room is always kept locked,' he told her. 'We're careful to keep the windows shut as well.' He looked at her gravely. 'One morning when Miss Cunningham, the biology teacher, opened up and came in here she found every animal dead. And it was the way in which they were dead,' he said quietly, shaking her head. 'Some were torn to pieces, others had drowned. It was a most horrible sight.'

'And Gideon did it?' Theresa said incredulously.

'We didn't know at first. We couldn't work out how it could have happened. But then some of the other children reported that Gideon had told them he had done it. Apparently he had been boasting of it. I questioned him, of course, and he didn't deny it. He wouldn't tell me how he had got the key. It seemed impossible. Miss Cunningham had one and the caretaker had the other. We never had any proof.'

Theresa looked at him quickly. That was what Phil had said: *No proof.*

'He must have frightened those animals out of their wits,' Mr Franks said. 'Some of them had torn themselves to pieces.' He looked around the room. 'Others had battered themselves against the bars of their cages. There is no doubt that they had been petrified.'

'But are you sure?' Theresa said.

Mr Franks looked at her. 'He as good as admitted it to me. On the day before it happened there had been some trouble in a biology class. Gideon had been misbehaving. Nothing very serious, really. But Miss Cunningham, who had taken the class, had punished Gideon in a minor way – I think she gave him a detention, or something like that, nothing very extraordinary. When I spoke to him about this afterwards it was apparent to me that he hated Miss Cunningham, hated her with a virulence that I've never seen in a child before. This thing that happened with the animals was some kind of revenge. Miss Cunningham swore that when she gave Gideon the detention he had said that he would "get her back". Those, I believe, were his very words. So, putting all this together, there really seems to be no doubt. I called in your father and told him that I couldn't keep Gideon at the school.'

When Theresa left the school she was subdued and pensive. There was little doubt in her mind that Gideon was capable of destroying the animals; after all, he had killed the goldfish. She herself had heard him admit it. As she walked along she tried to put the pieces of the jigsaw together, without much success. Yes, he could kill animals. 'And people?' she wondered. She had seen him look with such hatred at people. When he was thwarted, when he didn't get his own way, she had seen him consumed with loathing. She knew all that was true. But Phil's story, his suggestion that Gideon had controlled his mind . . . Surely that was impossible. But how had he got into that biology room? She was sceptical about the story of the key. Naturally, to Mr Franks, that seemed the best explanation. That was the rational thing to believe. But Gideon couldn't have got hold of the key. She was almost sure that he hadn't. Even Mr Franks had admitted that it was almost impossible.

But if you didn't accept the rational explanation, what were you left with? She shuddered. What you were left with was this 'special power' that Phil had spoken of. Did Gideon have special power, the power over people's minds? It seemed incredible, so incredible that she could hardly imagine it. There must be some other explanation. And so she walked along, deep in thought, but unable to come up with any answers.

She went to the station and caught the train home. It was a long journey. She sat in the corner of the compartment, looking out of the window. The rhythm of the train lulled the whirling confusion of her thoughts. There were no answers, no answers. Her head fell back against the padded back of the seat. No answers. The train jogged on. She fell asleep.

Let yourself go, Theresa. A soft insistent voice in her head. *Let yourself go.* She was hanging on to a metal bar. The flat, grey surface of water. Bordering clumps of reeds. It was all still, perfectly quiet. Yet, as she slept, a horrible fear crept into her. There was something in that water. What it was she did not know. 'Daddy,' she whimpered in her sleep. 'Come back.' Before her was the water and behind her was the fire. She was struggling, clinging on with her fingers. She could see her bright painted nails, red with the varnish that Phil had given her, clawing against the metal bar. And then the voice again. *Let yourself go.*

'Daddy,' she was calling out. Then someone was shaking her by the arm. She struggled to awaken.

'Are you all right?' An elderly woman was peering into her face. 'You were having a bad dream, my dear. I thought I'd better wake you.'

'Yes,' Theresa said. 'A bad dream.' She smiled weakly up at the woman. 'Thank you,' she said. 'I'm all right now.'

The elderly woman went back to her seat on the other side of the compartment.

Theresa looked down at her own hands. She wasn't wearing any nail varnish today. In her dream her nails had been bright red. She frowned. There was something that she was trying to remember, but as yet it escaped her.

21

It had been a very long day, even longer than usual. Dr Richards sat in his room at Glendale feeling tired. He was about to take off his white overall and go home to his house, which adjoined the main building of the hospital, when something made him stop. There was something he ought to do before he left. He needed a preparation for the following morning for one of the patients. 'I'll just make it up before I go,' he said to himself.

Dr Richards had been rather depressed for a week or

two. The sad case of Nurse Simpson's death had been a shock to everyone at Glendale, and the tragedy of Williams had affected him as well. Apart from those two events, however, he was troubled. He was experiencing a lot of difficulty with the young boy, Gideon, and though he was an experienced doctor and had handled many bad cases during his long years at Glendale and other hospitals, there was something about Gideon which he had never encountered before. Not ever, as far as he could remember, had he been so adversely affected by a patient. Gideon made him feel extremely nervous, and that was unsettling.

He sat down at his desk and picked up the telephone. One of his children answered. Then his wife came to the phone. He was always late, she was used to it. 'How long will you be?' she asked.

'Not long,' he said. 'Half an hour at the most.' He heard her laugh. 'I mean it,' he insisted. 'It won't be an hour. It will be half an hour.' Then he put down the phone and sighed. He stretched himself. God, he was tired. 'Oh, I won't bother tonight,' he thought. 'They can make it up in the central pharmacy.' He didn't make up many of the prescriptions himself. He didn't know why he'd thought of doing it tonight. He got up from the desk and went over to the door of the adjoining room. There was one thing that he kept in the pharmacy that he thought he would take advantage of: a bottle of whisky. He stood in front of the bench, still thinking of Gideon. Most of the cases in this part of the hospital were fairly straightforward. Standard treatments, standard responses. Then he remembered Williams. What had gone wrong there? He took down a beaker and put it on the bench. Perhaps he should have had Williams transferred, perhaps he should have spotted he was relapsing. But it hadn't seemed that way and they had been keeping an eye on him. With his right hand he reached to the back of the top shelf. That's where he kept the whisky, right at the back, out of sight. He pulled out the stopper and went to pour it out. When he looked down he gasped in shock. 'My God,' he said to himself. He had taken down the wrong bottle. Concentrated hydrochloric acid. 'Phew,' he said. His hand was shaking. Once, when he was a student, he had been clumsy. He had splashed a few drops of it on the back of his hand. A long time ago but you could still see the little white scars where the hair had never grown. He had been especially careful since then, for the incident had horrified him. He could still remember the harsh stinging. He put the stopper back in the bottle and stood it on the bench.

'That would never do,' he said to himself. He gulped and thought of the burning acid going down his throat. He needed that whisky more than ever now. But as he reached up to take down the bottle the flap of his coat knocked over the acid bottle. With a jerking movement he stretched out his hand to stop it, but it was too late. The stopper flew out and the acid spurted over his hand. He let out a terrible scream, almost fainting with the pain. The surface of the skin was dissolving in the acid. Wisps of pungent steam rose up and filled his nostrils.

'I must put something on it,' he thought. 'An alkali to neutralise it.' But he was horribly shaken. He couldn't think clearly. He looked at the shelf. Which bottle was it? His eyes wouldn't focus. Where the hell was it? He staggered against the bench and felt the acid, which was still running off the edge, seep into his coat and begin to burn the flesh of his stomach. 'My God,' he screamed. 'What am I doing?' For he didn't seem to be in possession of his own faculties.

He reached forward with his hand. This bottle, that bottle. It must be one of them. He knocked the bottles awry, spilling more and more of the deadly contents. Fumes rose up into the surrounding air. '*Help*,' he screamed. But the room was cut off and far away from the corridor. No one heard him.

'If only I could get out of here,' he thought. But he seemed to have no will to move. When he looked down at his hand he could see the flesh peeling back, and through it the white bone. It shocked him to see the exposed bone of his own hand. A kind of panic came over him and he thrashed wildly about, not knowing what he was doing. He had always hated that terrible acid, but he had kept his feelings under control. Now the full force of his fear and loathing overcame him. '*Help me*,' he screamed out again. His voice was harsh with the pain which was rushing through his body. He was on his knees at the bench. The acid was splashing on to his face and he could feel the skin shrivelling and burning.

He struggled towards the sink. He must get to the water, at least. Pulling himself up, he turned on a tap and thrust his hands under the running water. Above the sink there was a mirror and he caught sight of his face in it. Horror came over him. One side of his cheek was flapping loose with the blood dripping from it. Part of his jaw was exposed. He could see the acid, even as he watched, searing deeper and deeper into the inner red flesh. In agony he splashed at his face with the water. But it brought no relief. The acid worked on, eating into him, cutting through the soft flesh. The pain was excruciating. He was beyond all reason.

'They mustn't see me,' he thought. He was in a mad frenzy. He staggered across to the door and closed it. No one must see him. The sight was too much. He was grinding his teeth together in the pain and rocking his head from side to side. He rushed about in the small room, knocking against the sink, the bench, the wall. More bottles were displaced. They rolled off the bench and shattered on the floor. He could feel the thick glass crunching against his shoes. And everywhere were the terrible fumes. Sulphur, fluorine and chlorine mingled together in a haze. He couldn't see and he could hardly breathe. And from him dripped blood. Both his hands, and his face, were now bleeding profusely.

He fell to his knees and immediately the acid on the floor soaked through the cloth of his trousers. He was being consumed by acid.

'*Ahhh.*' The sound was torn from his flaking lips. Was there no end to the pain? The flesh of one of his knees was gone now. He could feel the smooth white ball of bone pressing against the floor. The pain went on and on surging through him in ever greater waves. A tidal swell of agony that he could not contain.

He was slipping now, falling forward on to the wet floor. More bottles crashed around him from the bench above. He reached out a hand to save himself, but he had no strength left with which to move.

His eyes were closed. He couldn't struggle any more. Dimly, he was aware of the dissolving process. The flesh on his hands had almost gone. A dark wave of unconsciousness was rising up to take him. When he lifted his head for the last time his face had already taken on the appearance of a skeleton. But still a thread of life hung on, unwilling to be wiped away.

'He's repressing his feelings,' he thought, and somewhere inside him he knew that he was thinking of Gideon. 'But perhaps he doesn't care. Perhaps . . .' Somewhere he could hear laughter. It was a long way off. He thought of his wife. She'd be putting the children to bed. He tried to picture their faces but he could only see the face of the boy. The boy Gideon. 'I don't understand him,' he thought. 'I'm the doctor and I'm supposed to, but I don't understand him.' Again he heard the faint echo of distant laughter. A cruel sound. It washed over him, taking away the last vestige of his consciousness.

His body lay in the pool of acid, the flesh slowly

melting in the river of chemical fire.

22

Theresa sat by the bedside. She had told Phil about the incident at the school. He had listened in horror as she went into the details of what had happened.

'I want you to go away,' he said at last. 'I'm afraid for you. It would be safer if you went away for a while. Gideon could stay at Glendale for the time being.'

'There's something else as well,' she told him. Her voice was very subdued.

'What?' he asked her. He was tense. He knew from her voice that she had something unpleasant to tell him.

'I phoned the hospital this morning,' she said quietly. 'It's Dr Richards. Oh, Phil, there's been another accident. A terrible accident. Dr Richards is dead.'

Phil was silent for a moment. His face was dark. 'How did he die?' he finally asked.

'They found him covered in acids in his pharmacy. The little room adjoining his office where we looked that day. It was so horrible, Phil. His body . . . The nurse I spoke to said his body was practically eaten away by the chemicals.' Her voice began to choke. 'I've never heard of anything so awful. D'you think . . .? D'you think . . .?'

'Yes,' he said. 'I'm afraid I do. I think Gideon had something to do with it.'

'I've made up my mind, Phil,' Theresa said. 'I'm going to see him this afternoon. I must speak to him. I must find out for certain if he is involved in all this.'

'He wouldn't admit it, would he?' Phil said.

Theresa looked angry. 'I'll get it out of him,' she said.

'No,' Phil said. 'I don't want you to go. You mustn't go

near him. If what we suspect is true, he's dangerous. You don't know what he might do in revenge.'

Theresa slumped back. 'But what *do* we suspect? We have no evidence for anything.'

Lying back in the bed, Phil stared up at the ceiling. His brow furrowed as he concentrated. 'Gideon thought I suspected something,' he said. 'And, anyway, he's always disliked me. But that afternoon at the hospital, when I was there, it's true, I did suspect him of something. And he knew that. I'm sure of it. You should have seen the way he looked at me.' Phil shook his head. 'I know he always stares, but this was different. There was something in his eyes. Then, that night, I thought I was being attacked by rats.' He shook his head again, this time more vigorously. 'It wasn't just that I thought it. It was stronger than that. It was real to me. It was just like a real experience. Even now, I find it hard to believe that it didn't really happen. I could feel them biting me.' He laughed grimly. 'I was lucky. I fell in front of the train, but all I got was a fractured pelvis and a few cracked ribs.' His eyes narrowed. He was trying to put things together. 'Gideon got inside my mind,' he said. 'Anyone who gets in his way, anyone he dislikes . . .' He looked at Theresa and then tried to sit forward, but he was restrained by the plaster cast. 'He's trying to use you,' he said.

'I know what you say seems like an explanation,' Theresa said, 'but isn't it a little far-fetched?'

'How do you explain it?' Phil asked her.

'All these deaths could be a series of coincidences,' she said. 'And what happened to you . . . You had been drinking.' She knew it didn't sound convincing.

'You don't believe in coincidences like that do you? And I wasn't that drunk. I told you.'

Theresa shrugged. 'There is something strange going on,' she said. 'But Gideon won't hurt me, even if what you surmise is true.'

'What about your parents?' Phil said grimly.

Theresa's face broke up and she was close to tears. Her voice was low. 'He wouldn't kill his own parents, would he? If you say he needs me, didn't he need them? Didn't he need them to look after him?'

'I've thought about that,' Phil said. 'I've done nothing much else but think while I've been lying here. Perhaps he made a mistake. Even if he has got powers . . . special powers . . . he's still only a child. Something makes him angry and he retaliates. He may not always be able to predict what will happen. Things may get beyond his control. That's why you could be in danger. If you made him angry, there's no telling what he might do. Please, Theresa, don't go and see him. Stay away from him.'

'I can't,' Theresa said. 'Supposing all this is rubbish. Supposing he is just an innocent child. Anyway,' she said, thinking. 'If he *did* have this special power, wouldn't he be even more angry if I didn't go and see him?'

'I'll be out of here in a couple of weeks,' Phil said. 'We could go away.'

'I must find out,' Theresa insisted.

Phil sighed. He was tired and his body ached. 'Oh well,' he said. 'I suppose he *might* be more angry if he doesn't see you. You have a point there. But please be careful. Don't confront him too openly.'

For a while they sat side by side on the bed holding hands, bewildered and confused.

'I told him about your accident,' Theresa said.

'Did he say anything?' Phil asked her.

'Not a thing. And he gave no sign, either. But you know how he is, how uncommunicative he can be.'

'Yes,' Phil said.

Theresa pressed her hands against her eyes. 'I'm so tired,' she said.

'You're over-tense,' Phil said.

'I've been having nightmares,' Theresa told him. 'Or at

least, I feel it's *one* nightmare and I keep seeing fragments of it. And curiously, it's all familiar to me. I don't know what I mean exactly, but I feel I know that dream. As soon as I wake up I forget most of the details.' She frowned, narrowing her eyes. 'I'm trying to remember,' she said. 'There's something about the fire, but it's all so confused and indistinct.'

Lifting up his hand, Phil stroked the back of her head. 'Your hair is growing longer,' he said. 'As soon as I get out of here I'm going to take you away for a few weeks.'

Theresa could tell from the tone of his voice that he meant, 'I'm going to take you away forever.'

'Let's get married straight away,' he said. 'Let's make a new life where we can forget about everything that's happened.'

'I only wish it was possible,' she said.

'We can,' he told her.

'There's still Gideon,' she reminded him, and the name hung over them like an ominous black cloud.

They discussed again whether all their fears could be true, going over and over the same ground. They didn't reach any conclusion.

'I've got to go now,' Theresa said, and they both had fear in their eyes.

'You don't have to see him,' Phil said once more. 'Why don't you go to the police and tell them what's happened?'

Theresa smiled at him. 'What could I tell them?' she said. 'What could I tell them that they would ever believe? That my brother is some kind of devil who makes people destroy themselves?' She shook her head. 'No one would ever believe us, Phil. We're not even sure that we believe ourselves, are we?'

Phil held on to her hand. 'I don't want you to go,' he repeated.

Theresa withdrew her hand. 'I've got to,' she said. 'You

do see, don't you?'

'Yes,' he admitted. 'But I still don't like it. It's not even as if we can go together. You've got to face him on your own.'

Theresa laughed. A high, shrill and rather false sound. 'We're the ones who are crazy, Phil. I'm going to visit my brother. He's had a bad shock, a horrible experience. He's upset and disoriented. That's all there is to it.' She leant down and kissed Phil's cheek. 'Isn't that the truth?' she said.

He laughed mirthlessly with her. 'It's one kind of truth,' he agreed.

23

The day-room was very quiet. There was hardly any conversation, and an atmosphere of gloom hung over everything. Gideon sat by the window in his usual seat, watching the drive for Theresa's arrival. At last, he saw her passing between the trees, coming nearer. He watched in silence, without making a move. There was something in the manner of her walk that made him fearful. He clutched the side of the chair. She was going to try and stop him from going home. He sensed it. She'd been talking to that Phil again. But he would soon change her mind. She was weak, he would force her to let him go home. He wasn't going to stay here any longer. Nobody was going to stop him from leaving, not even Theresa. He screwed up his face in a petulant frown. She'd better not try and tell *him* what to do. She was close now, so close that she might see him. He turned away from the window, not wanting to catch her eye.

'Hello, Gideon.' Her manner was sober.

Gideon looked at her sharply, and without returning her greeting said, 'Am I going home today?'

'Not today,' she said, and though he waited she offered no explanation.

'Why not?' he demanded at length. 'Why am I not going home today?' He stared at her with a cold expression on his face.

'Well . . .' she began. 'We've got to have a talk. Just you and me.' She held up a key. 'I asked the staff nurse if we could go down by the lake and she said it would be all right.'

'All right, Theresa,' Gideon said. 'But I want to go home today. Do you understand?'

'You can't always have what you want,' she said tersely, but she avoided his eye.

He was furious. She was challenging him. Well, she wouldn't win. He *would* get his own way.

Suddenly, Theresa looked down at him, forgetting her fear. 'You've got to remember, Gideon, that I'm your only relative,' she said. Then in a voice almost mysterious she added, 'You need me. Do *you* understand that?'

Inside, Gideon was raging with fury but outwardly he was calm. What did she mean by all this? What was she up to? Well, she'd better be careful. Then he remembered her words, *I'm your only relative*. His face clouded over. It was hateful, but it was true – he *did* need her. While he was a child he needed her. 'But it's only for a few years,' he thought to himself. 'One day I'll get my own back for all this.' Smiling, he said to Theresa, 'Let's go for a walk, then.' He even took hold of her hand to make her happy. He had to keep her happy, that was all. If he did that, she would let him do what he wanted. He knew Theresa, she was soft.

They walked out through the doors of the day-room on to the dry summer lawn. It was brown and patchy in places where it had become scorched during the hottest days.

'Do you want to sit down?' Gideon asked Theresa, doing his best to cover his hostility and please her.

'No, we won't sit here,' she said. 'We're going to the lake.'

'Oh yes,' he said, smiling at her warmly.

She felt quite hot and restless as they walked through the gardens, and this wasn't just the effect of the weather. It was caused by Gideon. She *knew* he was up to something. She could tell. The way he was holding her hand . . . It was completely out of character. Normally, Gideon hated touching anyone. She was irritated to think that he imagined she would be so easy to fool.

'It's nice by the lake,' Gideon said. 'I went there the other day . . .' No, he mustn't mention Nurse Simpson. That would be a mistake. And he mustn't mention fish and remind her of the goldfish. He had to be careful, he had to be on his guard. She wanted to find out things. He bit his lip in exasperation. There were so many things to remember, so many things that he mustn't say. 'It's a nice afternoon,' he said in a cheerful voice.

'Yes, isn't it,' Theresa said with irony in her voice. He really must take her for a fool. She glanced down at him walking beside her and almost at once she felt a sense of misgiving. Perhaps she was being ungenerous. After all, as she had said to Phil, he *might* be innocent. It *was* possible. She mustn't make the mistake of judging him too hastily. That would be awful. Maybe he was merely trying to be pleasant. Perhaps he was fond of her. The thought made her quiver slightly. She looked at him again. The sun was catching the ends of his hair, making them seem golden. In fact, he looked quite angelic. His dark round eyes seemed to contain no evil at that moment and the fair curls hung around his forehead, giving his face a gentle look.

Gideon saw her watching him, noticed the softened

line of her face. 'Good,' he thought, and he was pleased. He was taking her in. She would do whatever he wanted. He gave her a radiant smile. 'Theresa,' he said. 'I'm so looking forward to coming home.' He squeezed her hand.

Theresa was confused. She had started out feeling hard against him but now, now . . . She just wasn't sure any more. Perhaps it was all far-fetched nonsense. Even the thought of Phil seemed distant at that moment. She could hardly picture his face. Everything seemed distant except Gideon beside her. He was smiling at her, and she returned the smile.

'I'm looking forward to coming home,' he repeated.

Home. The word echoed in her head. *Home*. And suddenly she started, the word liberating her from Gideon's power. For home meant the old house. Her face flinched as she remembered the fire. An image of the flames and her father's hand reaching out, trying to escape, flashed through her mind.

Gideon saw the change in her, and he was angry. He'd nearly got her, but she had escaped him.

'We've got to talk,' she said, rather severely. 'I wanted to go to the lake so we could be alone. I don't want anyone to overhear what I've got to say.'

'All right, Theresa.' Gideon's voice was small but hard. 'Anything you say.'

She unlocked the gate in the fence and they passed through. Down the gravelled path to the lake.

'We'll sit down here,' Theresa said, when they reached a bench.

And Gideon smiled to himself. It was the bench where he had sat with Nurse Simpson.

Theresa stared for a moment across the parkland. In the distance she could see the surrounding high wall. It gave her confidence to know that he couldn't get away. For though they were outside the gardens at Glendale, they were still within the precincts of the hospital.

'I went to see Mr Franks,' she began. She felt Gideon stiffen beside her. 'Well,' she said. 'Did you hear me?' But this time Gideon did not answer. 'Tell me how you got into the biology room,' she said in a matter of fact voice. She wasn't going to waste time asking him if he was guilty. When she turned to look at Gideon she saw that he was staring at her. She had never seen a look of such implacable hatred. There was no pretence in him now, no pretence of friendship and affection. 'Tell me,' she insisted.

Gideon's lips were set in a firm line and he did not speak.

'What happened to Dr Richards?' Her heart was beating fast. She was coming at last to see, beyond any doubt, that Gideon was implicated. He denied nothing, his guilt was written all over him. 'And what did you do to Phil?' she said. 'He nearly died. You're quiet now, you've got nothing to say now.'

Gideon stood up.

'Until you give some sort of explanation you can't come home.' She enunciated each word clearly. 'I'm going to talk to the doctors,' she said. 'I'm going to tell them what happened at the school . . . and everything.'

'You're mad,' he finally said. 'They'll think you're crazy. They'll lock you up. How could *I* have done those things?'

Neither of them moved.

Deep inside her head Theresa could feel a movement of fear. She was staring at the lake. 'The water,' she muttered.

She heard Gideon laugh. 'The water,' he repeated.

The lake stretched out before her, a grey unbroken wash of water. Reeds at the edges. The sight made her feel quite weak. 'Tell me,' she said again, but her voice was practically inaudible.

'Hot, isn't it?' Gideon said in a contemptuous voice. But he too was frightened. He knew now that Theresa would not help him. She had guessed too much. She wouldn't have him to live with her. He could release the dark forces in the recesses of her mind, he could make her destroy herself as he had the others. But he could not make her help him. 'You're frightened of the water, aren't you?' he said.

Theresa's eyes were fixed on the surface of the water. For a moment she was almost drawn into it. Then she wrenched herself round to face him. 'The fire.' She forced herself to say the words. Somehow she knew that she *must* say them, knew instinctively that those words, and only those, would have any effect on Gideon. 'The fire,' she said again. 'The fire.'

And, amazingly, he shrank back as though he could feel the very heat of the scorching flames.

'What happened that night?' Her voice was stronger. She felt a surge of hatred go through her. If he had started the fire, if he had burnt the house, if he had killed her mother and father . . . 'What happened?' she demanded.

Gideon's face had gone white. He could feel the words coming into his mind, the words that would tell her everything. She mustn't know, she must never find out. He sensed that in some strange way she was dangerous to him. In the release of her hatred and anger there was a power that was greater than his own. She didn't know she had that power, he must not let her find it. Afraid that he would speak, afraid that he would reveal too much, he turned and ran.

'Gideon,' she called. 'Gideon!'

As he ran, his face was grim. He had to get her. It was essential. But not now, not here. He couldn't be locked up in this place. He had to get away from here. But he would get her. He would have his revenge.

24

After Theresa told the nurses that Gideon had run off, she waited at Glendale for an hour or two to see if they would find him. Every part of the grounds was searched but there was no sign of him, and eventually the police were informed of his escape.

'You might as well go home,' a doctor said. 'There's no point in waiting here any longer.'

Theresa nodded. 'I'll phone later on this evening,' she said.

'It's most unfortunate,' the doctor said, shaking his head. 'But I wouldn't worry too much. The police will soon find him.'

It was early evening by the time she left, and she went straight to see Phil.

'But why would he run off like that?' Phil said.

'He was afraid of me. I can't think why. But I could sense that he was.'

'You mean, afraid of what you were going to do? Afraid that you were going to tell the doctors and the police?'

Theresa shook her head slowly. 'Oh no,' she said. 'He was angry about that, but there was something else. It was *me* he seemed to be frightened of.'

'The police will pick him up,' Phil said.

'Yes,' Theresa agreed, but neither of them was really convinced.

They were both depressed, wondering how it would all end. They hardly spoke. At last, Theresa got up to go.

'I'll come and see you tomorrow afternoon,' she said. 'I'm going to Mrs MacKenzie's in the morning.'

'I feel so helpless stuck here,' Phil complained. 'I wish I could be with you.'

'I wish you could too,' she said.

The fears that they both felt were unspoken, but as Theresa was leaving Phil called out, 'Please be careful.'

That night Theresa found it difficult to sleep. She was restless and lay on the bed tossing and turning. Each time she dozed off, her sleep was disturbed and broken. Inside her mind she could feel the tendrils of some dark and unfathomable abomination stretching up to claim her. And as she fought against its domination fragmented images flickered before her. She saw Gideon's face, angry and full of hatred, monstrous. Then frightened, just a child. Wide-eyed and innocent. She saw the stretch of grey water, the flames of the fire.

Once, she woke up completely. It was the middle of the night and pitch-black outside. She got up from the bed and stood by the window. In the sky above, a vast swarm of stars dotted the dark blue expanse. Everything was still and deathly quiet. Below the sky the shadowed buildings stood in geometric grimness, reaching upwards. A spire, chimneys, sloping roofs.

Theresa shivered. Her eyes were heavy with fatigue. 'Why is he so frightened of me?' she wondered. But she had no energy to pursue the thought, so she went back to bed and drifted once more into uncertain sleep.

She was up early the next morning, glad to leave her bed behind. She took a long time getting ready. 'I look awful,' she thought, as she looked in the mirror. Her eyes were drawn and tired, and her skin grey. She washed her hair and put on her make-up and painted the nails of her fingers. She knew that Mrs MacKenzie liked to see her looking well, so she made a special effort. She put on her brightest dress and her new silk scarf. The grim face in the mirror hardly seemed to match the cheerful colours of her clothing.

Before she left she phoned Glendale, but there was no word about Gideon. 'I'll talk to the doctors this afternoon,' she thought, as she put the phone down. 'I'll tell them everything, even if they do think I'm mad.'

When Mrs MacKenzie opened the door of her cottage, the first thing she said was, 'You look so tired, Theresa. Aren't you sleeping properly? But what a lovely dress!' She led Theresa into her little sitting-room.

It was a beautiful morning. The windows were thrown open and the warm sunlit air, heavy with the scent of stocks and sweet williams, drifted into the room.

Mrs MacKenzie made Theresa a cup of coffee, and the two of them sat together on the couch.

'I can tell something's wrong,' Mrs MacKenzie said. 'You tell me what it is.'

Theresa hesitated. She didn't want to upset the old lady too much. She didn't know what to tell her. At last she said, 'It's Gideon. You know he's in that hospital, at Glendale . . .'

Mrs MacKenzie nodded.

'Well,' Theresa continued. 'He wants to come and live with me at the flat. At first I wanted him to, but now I'm not sure. He seems so disturbed.' She sighed. 'And he's run away, disappeared from the hospital. The police are looking for him, but he hasn't turned up anywhere as yet.'

Mrs MacKenzie looked agitated. 'I don't think you should have him to live with you, my dear. I don't like to say unkind things about him, but I might as well be honest. You know I've never really liked him. He's always been a strange and rather unkind little boy. And those goldfish,' she said, clicking her tongue. 'I wouldn't have believed that possible. I really think that hospital is the best place for him.' She took Theresa's hand. 'You mustn't be upset by what *I* say. I only want you to be happy.' She smiled at Theresa with fond indulgence. 'You've got a nice young man. It wouldn't be fair to him to have Gideon with you, not after you're married. He would only make trouble.' There was a pause, and then she continued in a sharp voice, 'There's something wrong with him, I've always known it. Your poor mother always tried . . .' Her eyes were filled with tears and Theresa had to comfort her.

Suddenly Mrs MacKenzie looked straight into Theresa's eyes. 'I hope you'll forgive me, my dear, if I say something in confidence to you. I don't want to bring back unhappy memories, but I feel I've got to tell you.'

Theresa began to shake. Mrs MacKenzie was going to talk about the fire. She could tell by the look in her eyes.

'I didn't say anything to the police about this. At the time I was too shaken to be sure of anything. But now you're talking about having Gideon to live with you . . . My mind's a lot clearer than it was on that night, Theresa.'

'What happened?' Theresa asked.

The old lady took a deep breath. 'Well,' she began. 'When I woke up, my room was already full of smoke. I got to the outside door, and when I opened it I saw that the house was a mass of flames. I stood at the top of the steps for a while, too shocked to move. That was before I telephoned. And then, when I was standing there, I saw Gideon. He came out of the front door.' Her voice was shocked at the memory. 'He wasn't running. He walked out of the door and closed it behind him, as casual as you like.'

Theresa looked away. She was trying to remember. Yes, the front door had been closed.

'And then,' the old lady continued, 'he walked over to that big clump of bushes on the drive. You know, the laurels. Then he turned round and looked back at the house. He just stood there watching the flames. And, Theresa, he was smiling. I could see his face quite clearly. That's when I ran back into my rooms and telephoned for the fire brigade. And after that I ran down the steps – that's when I met you – and I didn't notice him again. No,' she said, considering, 'I never saw him after that. But I remember his face very well. He looked . . . pleased with himself.' The old lady shook herself. 'No, you mustn't have him to live with you, Theresa. It would be wrong.'

They both looked at one another, each knowing in their hearts that Gideon had started the fire.

'You've got to keep away from him,' Mrs MacKenzie said.

'No one knows where he is.' Theresa's voice was almost a whisper. She was still thinking of that night, that terrible night. And inside her was a growing hatred. She tried to subdue it, to avoid it, to pretend that it didn't exist. But it did, and it was becoming stronger.

25

It had been easy getting away from the hospital. Gideon had run into the trees and then followed the wall. It was too high for him to climb. Eventually, he had come to the rear gate-house. The pair of large gates were closed, but a side gate was open. Beside it stood the gatekeeper. He was a tall, big-boned man, and it seemed impossible that Gideon would ever get past him.

The boy walked out from the trees and approached the gate.

'Hello, sonny,' the gateman said in a friendly voice. 'What are you doing here? Got lost, have you?'

Gideon's eyes slowly dilated until the black pupils seemed to swell out and contain everything.

The gateman looked down at him. 'I'd better phone in and ask what to do with you,' he said. 'Come along in here with me.' He indicated the little lodge which stood next to the gates. But as he went to turn, he faltered and then stood as if transfixed. His body stiffened and he lifted a hand as if he would ward off some invisible danger.

The man had been in the navy when he was young and now he was back in the sea again. The ship was going down. He was trapped below the deck. Through the swirling smoke he could hear the screams of the other men dying. The water was rising inexorably, now it was covering his head. He couldn't breathe. As he stood by the gate he gasped for breath. The darkness beneath the water obscured his vision and he could see nothing.

Gideon walked out through the gate.

A few moments later, the gateman reeled back into consciousness. His body was racked with coughing. He looked in front of him and saw only the path, the bushes and the trees. He peered around for the boy who had been standing there, but of him there was no sign.

'They'll never find me,' Gideon thought, as he walked along. 'They'll never catch me, they'll never lock me up again.' But he was not at ease. 'I've made mistakes,' he thought. 'It shouldn't have been like this.' He bit his lip, thinking of his errors. He had been wrong to let anger get the better of him. 'A few more years,' he thought to himself, 'and I wouldn't have needed anybody.' He had been too hasty.

That night, he found an empty house, broke a window at the back and climbed in. The house was damp and silent, but he didn't mind. He liked being on his own. He hated other people, hated them near him. Sitting in one of the bedrooms he leant back against a wall and thought about what had happened and tried to plan what he would do. Sometimes he ranted like a spoilt child in a temper tantrum. He wanted things his own way. At other times he thought clearly and carefully about the mistakes he had made. Once, when it was quite dark, he heard footsteps on the pavement outside, and when he looked down from the window he saw a man walking his dog. Gideon opened his mind to the dark currents of that other consciousness, twisting himself down in the subterranean depths. He exulted in the special power that he had. Yes, he could make them frightened. He could open the flood-gates of their subliminal fears. He dipped into the shallows of the dog's thoughts and laughed when he heard the animal howl and the man scream out. Then Gideon withdrew, smiling to himself as the man ran away down the road.

The night stretched away and he hardly slept. Gideon couldn't remember ever sleeping much. He would lie awake in the darkness, watching other people's minds, shaping and denying dreams. He could lift up their night-mares and make their flesh crawl. He liked the night best, for it was then that people's defences were down and their minds were like open safes to be plundered.

The darkness was broken by a vivid dawn, bright orange and streaked with red. Then the disc of sun rose above the rooftops, and the room in which he had sat through the night was illuminated by the glowing rays. Through the window he could see the cloudless sky stretching away into the hazy distance. He felt small and lost. 'If only there was someone to look after me,' he whined. Then he despised himself for his weakness. He beat his fists against the floor. 'I don't need anyone,' he cried out loud. 'I'm all alone and I don't want anyone.' He closed his eyes. There were dark coils of an old, deepening fear within him. But he wasn't frightened. 'They'll never get me,' he whispered. But even so, he shivered, and when he tried to look forward into the days ahead he could see nothing.

'Theresa will tell the doctors,' he thought. He was forcing himself to keep calm. He could feel the heat of spite prickling within him but he fought it back. That was not the way to act, not now. Now he had to remain cool.

Yes. Theresa would tell the doctors everything she knew and everything she feared. There would be investigations. They would find out about the animals. Damn, he hated himself for doing that. He had acted like a kid and then boasted about it. Fancy boasting about it! He knew better now. Still, he was glad he'd paid that Miss Cunningham back. She'd asked for it.

His eyes blackened. Now he must get Theresa. They would investigate everything she told them and they would keep him locked up. He smiled with an evil leer that split his lips open, revealing the line of white teeth. He'd make them suffer.

Then his anger faded and dissolved. He was all alone. He must plan what he was going to do. First, he must settle things with Theresa. Then . . .then . . . He couldn't think. One thing at a time. First, Theresa.

He crept out of the empty house. It was still very early in the morning and there was hardly anyone about. He knew where Theresa was living now. He'd go there and wait for his opportunity.

For an hour or more, he stood in a doorway opposite her flat. Then when she came out he followed her, at a distance. Once or twice he concentrated his mind and tried to dip down into her thoughts, but there was a barrier there. A barrier of antipathy and anger. Yet he knew it was a fragile thing, that defence of hers. Gideon followed quietly and carefully. Her defences wouldn't last. Later, she would relax, give way. She would forget, and then . . .

He followed her to Mrs MacKenzie's, and when he saw the old woman open the door he grimaced. He hated that old woman. She was always interfering, poking her nose into things.

Scowling at the thought of Theresa gossiping with that garrulous old fool, Gideon crept forward. He opened the gate without a sound and slid into the garden. The window of the sitting-room was open and he could hear every word.

I've never really liked him . . .

The high, thin, reedy voice that he loathed. She had tried to befriend him once, with her wet eyes and her hands always reaching out to touch. He heard her talking about the dead goldfish and he nearly laughed out loud. He was glad he had killed them. Those tiny brains. He had whisked the cells into inchoate panic until the blood vessels had exploded in terror.

And, Theresa, he was smiling . . .

Gideon could hear the indignation in her voice. Indignation and dislike. But there was a thread of something else. She had always been frightened of him, and that was in her tone too.

You must not have him to live with you . . .

He hated her, hated her more than ever. He sat back in the shadow of the hedge and listened to them talking. Theresa and that odious old woman. He closed his eyes. Yes, Theresa was going to tell the doctors. He would have to stop her. And Mrs MacKenzie knew too much. And there was Phil in the hospital. Theresa must have told *him* everything. There was so much to do. There was Mr Franks at the old school. Theresa had been to talk to *him*. Was there no end to it? Gideon stifled a groan. His powers were not fully developed yet. If only he hadn't made so many mistakes! If only his mum and dad were still here to look after him, if only there was someone! He needed . . . There were tears of self-pity in his eyes. Then the self-pity turned, and flared into anger. That interfering old woman! She'd be the first . . .

As his mind twisted around his petulant loathing, he caught a glimpse of the anger in *Theresa's* mind. It matched his own. In that instant he wrenched all certainty from her thoughts and felt her mind stagger.

'I'll have to be going now, Mrs MacKenzie,' he heard her saying, and her voice was strained.

'But I thought you'd be staying for lunch.' Mrs MacKenzie pressed her. 'Can't you stay, my dear?' Then her voice trailed off.

'I must go,' Theresa said. 'I must.'

Gideon heard the rustle of their clothing as they stood up, and then the opening and closing of the front door. Then there was the sharp tapping of Theresa's shoes on the pavement as she walked away. He sat in the bushes staring towards the house. The old woman was alone.

26

After lunch, as Mrs MacKenzie was washing the dishes and putting them away, she noticed that the sky had suddenly darkened. 'It's going to rain,' she thought. 'I must bring in the clothes.' They were flapping wildly in the sudden stiff breeze, the clothes-line jerking up and down in a fast motion. 'There's going to be a storm.'

Fetching the basket from the scullery, she glanced out of the window and saw that birds were wheeling about in the sky. They were making a terrible noise too, squawking and cawing harshly in the rising wind. 'Yes,' she thought, 'a storm,' and slipping into her raincoat in case she should get wet, she went out into the garden to bring in the washing.

It was strangely dark and there was a peculiar yellowish light in the sky. As she reached the washing-line the first drops began to fall. Large flat splashes, against her forehead, her hands, the plastic raincoat. In a sudden gust of wind the line was lifted up beyond her reach. She struggled to get hold of it, but she could not quite manage to catch it. Each time she took a section of it in her hands the wind tugged it away from her with great force. The noise in the air about her was deafening. It was the birds. She looked around her fearfully, looked up into the darkened sky. She hated birds, hated them. Especially when they were unsettled like this. Now, they were veering about in the sky and making a dreadful noise.

Mrs MacKenzie grappled with the washing-line, slowly filling up her basket with the clothes. The rain was coming faster now, and already her hair was becoming damp. At last she had everything off the line, and she hurried back to the cottage, quite out of breath and in a nervous state because of the birds overhead.

She made herself a cup of tea, and when she next looked out of the window she saw that the birds were settling on the bushes at the end of the garden and on the distant lines of trees. More seemed to be coming all the time, wheeling high in the air and then joining the others on the swaying branches of the trees. They were still making an awful racket, and she closed the window in the kitchen so that she would not be able to hear them.

Going back into her sitting-room at the rear of the cottage, Mrs MacKenzie noticed that there was a row of birds perched on the washing-line. Menacing they looked, the squat black bodies clinging to the swaying rope. And as they swung to and fro with the jerking movement of the line, the horrible, shrill dinning was kept up. Her heart beat a little faster. They seemed so close to the house. She wished they would go away. 'If only the weather would clear,' she thought. 'They'd fly away if the storm passed.'

But the storm did not pass. It hung in the air, never quite breaking and yet not dispersing, either. It was grey and gloomy and the whipping wind tore at the bushes and flowers in the garden, tossing them from one side to the other, bowing them to the earth, shaking off blossoms and petals, which flew up into the air and scattered across the gardens.

Mrs MacKenzie shivered. The atmosphere outside was heavy and oppressive. The wind seemed to be pressing everything down and the sky, like a great leaden weight, hung over everything. And on the trees and the tops of bushes, the washing-line and the fences which surrounded the garden, sat the rows of birds. They appeared to be watching. It made her grow quite cold to see them.

She went to the window, intending to draw the curtains – so that she would not have to see the awful sight of the birds, and to try and deaden the shrill sound they were making. As she took hold of the cloth to pull the first curtain across, she got the biggest shock she had ever had in her life.

Outside the window, in the lightly falling rain, stood Gideon. She put her hand to her heart to try and stay the wild beating inside her. He was there, right outside the glass. She had not seen him come into view, but she was not imagining his presence. She stood by the window, afraid to move. Her legs felt paralysed by his stare. She clung desperately to the edge of the curtain. 'Go away,' she muttered softly. 'Go away!' But instead of fulfilling her wish he came even closer to the window.

It was horrifying to the old woman. Gideon was now standing with his face pressed against the glass. His features were distorted and flattened, yet she could see the leering smile on his lips. And his eyes! They were blacker and deeper than she had ever seen them, and they were staring at her, fixedly, pinning her feet to the ground. There was such power in his eyes.

'I must not show him I'm afraid of him,' Mrs MacKenzie thought. 'That's what he wants, to terrify me.' So, forcing herself to seem calm and unruffled by his presence, she leant forward, and with a shaking hand opened the catch of the window. 'Oh, it's you, Gideon,' she said, trying to speak in an ordinary voice. 'Why ever are you standing out there in the rain?' Undaunted by his continuing silence she said again, 'Why are you standing in the garden? Come round to the kitchen door. I'll let you in. You don't want to get wet. You just missed Theresa. She was here a little while ago.'

Gideon drew his face back an inch. He was laughing. 'Oh, was she?' he said.

Mrs MacKenzie gasped. How long had he been standing there? Had he been watching her, without her realising it? Had he been there in the morning when Theresa was with her? It was a horrible thought, but she wouldn't put it past him. He was laughing. Horrible, cold laughter. Unnatural. Not like a child's. He was an unnatural boy. 'I'll have to phone the police,' she thought. 'As soon as I can, I'll ring them up.'

'I know what you're thinking.' Gideon's voice was spitefully gleeful. 'You just thought of phoning the police, didn't you?'

Mrs MacKenzie's heart missed a beat or two. 'Of course I didn't,' she lied.

Suddenly Gideon's face became grim. 'You hate me. You think I don't know, but I do.'

She looked at him aghast. He was smiling again now. 'You hate me,' he repeated.

'Go away,' she suddenly cried out. 'Get out of here!' All her dislike of him entered into her words. 'Go away or I *will* call the police.' She shook her fist at him.

'Mrs MacKenzie hates me,' he crooned. He was taunting her, and enjoying every minute of it. He made a face at her through the window, pressing his lips hard against the glass in a parody of a kiss. Flattened pink lips, slightly parted, revealing even teeth. Then he withdrew, and without saying another word he turned and walked unhurriedly out of the garden.

She heard the slam of the side gate and the sound of his retreating footsteps. 'Thank God,' she whispered. 'Thank God he's gone.' She was badly shaken and she had to sit down in an armchair to recover her equanimity. The awful experience seemed to draw all the energy out of her, and no sooner had she sat on the chair than she fell asleep, in a kind of painful exhaustion.

The sound of breaking glass woke her. She leapt immediately to her feet. It was now quite dark outside. She must have been asleep for a long time. What was that noise? It seemed to be coming from an upstairs room. Perhaps she had left a window open and the wind had smashed it. 'What a nuisance,' she thought, going into the hall. It had gone very quiet now, not a sound to be heard. Slowly she made her way up the staircase.

When she opened the door of her bedroom the most horrifying sight she had ever seen met her eyes. The room was full of birds. Crows and rooks perched on the bedstead and around the room – on the picture rail, the top of the wardrobe, and on the tops of cupboards, starlings and thrushes and tiny sparrows, crouched menacingly.

She let out a cry of terror, and the sound which escaped her lips seemed to bring them to life. They all flew up, and more came in through the jagged gaping window. It was all a wild flurry of feathers and a shrill cacophony of noise.

Gathering her wits, she grabbed the door handle. But they were too fast for her. Three black crows descended on her arm and began pecking at her wrist. She let the handle go in a scream of pain, and rushed back on to the landing. But they were after her, pursuing her down the narrow stairs. From below came the sound of splintering glass, followed by a thundering crash, and as she reached the bottom of the staircase a whole flock of gulls flew into the hall from the sitting-room and the dining-room and the kitchen. They made a weird shrieking noise which chilled her to the very bone.

And it was there in the hall that she met her death. Her heart seemed to rise up inside her, seemed to burst in her throat. Blood gushed from her mouth and she sank down to the floor. Blood, like a frothing wash of effluent, spread itself across her face and seeped into her summer dress. As she lay there, fast losing consciousness, the gulls pecked at her scalp, tore strips of flesh from her body, ripped into the skin of her face with their curved yellow beaks.

Then the crows came. They took her hair, strand by strand, wrenching it from her head with sharp tugs. And the sparrows and other small birds settled on her legs and feet, each finding some small portion of her to satisfy their lust. Even the robins, the most loved of birds, feasted upon her, pulling up the sinews and veins within her flesh, twisting them like worms upon their tiny but rapacious beaks.

The eyes, too, were not overlooked. Beaks of many colours and sizes pecked into her lids and into the moist hidden centres. They would leave nothing. And the air about the dying woman was rent with the sound of the squabbling, screaming birds. They were ravenous, furious, their eyes glazed with murderous intent.

She was dead. Her body sprawled in the dark hallway, racked and twisted by her last agonies of pain and fear.

27

Theresa walked aimlessly about the town, her mind spinning and thoughts tumbling through her head. She walked along one street which was crowded with people, then she turned off and was in a deserted avenue where her footsteps echoed. In a desultory way she kept looking out for Gideon, but without much hope of finding him, or even knowing whether she wanted to.

'I should go and see Phil,' she thought. She had promised to go that afternoon, but somehow she could not, and so she continued her lonely wandering.

Mrs MacKenzie's words kept coming back to her, throbbing inside her head. *He was smiling.* And the memory of those words made Theresa feel sick.

'He started the fire,' Theresa thought. There was a kind of rage inside her that burnt as fiercely as bright flames. Sometimes it leapt up, consuming her, and she walked faster, her feet keeping time with her angry feelings. But then her anger broke into disconnected fragments and she looked around her as though she was lost.

It began to rain, and the damp summer shower, warm and cloying, drenched her, so that wisps of hair clung to the sides of her face.

She passed by the police station and thought of going in, but really, what could she say? How could she explain to them what had happened?

Once or twice, when her mind seemed wreathed in black smoke, she could sense something of Gideon inside her mind. A thread of coldness, an invidious intrusion touching the depths of her thoughts. That made her angry, and she talked inside her head as if he was there, listening to her. And when she did that, the soft, strange touch retreated and was gone, and she was left with the feeling that water had seeped away through her fingers.

At one moment, as she stood in a shop doorway watching the drifts of rain on the grey tarmac, she thought she heard screaming and an echoing laugh. But when she looked round there was nothing there.

The shower passed over and the sun broke through, a clear shaft of light drying the pavements and throwing brilliant rainbow colours on to the leaves.

Theresa walked on, past the houses and shops, the offices and the churches. It felt as if she had some destination, but she was unaware of the factors which made her choose this street instead of that, guided her feet at the crossroads and led her eventually to the gates of the old city park.

She walked past the towering gates of the zoo and out on to the wide lawns which surrounded the tall brick walls of the zoo's boundary. She had walked for miles and now she was tired.

'Why have I come here?' she wondered. There seemed to be no good reason, nor, now, any reason to go anywhere else. She sat down on a seat at the foot of an oak tree. The leaves above her glistened with rain and occasionally the droplets fell down on to the ground below. Across the grass she could see the walls of the zoo and, beyond, the white buildings. In a kind of daze Theresa stared ahead of her. The sun beat down, drawing the moisture from the grass. Tiny plumes of steam rose upwards and then dissipated in the air. How long she sat there she had no idea. People walked past her, families going to the zoo, children chattering and laughing, but she did not notice.

'I'm waiting,' she thought, but she did not know exactly what for.

In the distance was a drone of traffic on the ring road,

and occasionally came the roar of a lion or the trumpeting of an elephant, but she did not hear them.

'Hello, Theresa.'

When she half turned on the seat she saw Gideon. He was smiling at her, but the smile was not kind. It held only contempt and the certainty of victory.

'You were waiting for me,' Gideon said.

'Yes,' Theresa replied quietly, though she had not known that he would come.

'Of course you were.' Gideon's voice sounded strange, not like a child's, not like a boy's. It was deeper than she remembered. It was the voice of a stranger, someone she did not know.

'I've got to look after myself,' Gideon said. He was quite matter of fact, speaking without emotion. 'I'm different from everyone else, you see. I've always known it, for as long as I can remember. Different.'

Theresa nodded. She accepted everything that he said. She seemed trance-like and acquiescent. Yet, somewhere inside her, was a thin ribbon of anger that rebelled against his quiet domination.

'I did want to live with you,' Gideon told her. 'It would have made things easier for me – for a few years, anyway.' The smile was set on his face in condescending mockery. 'But it's too late now. You'd stir everything up and you'd make so much trouble.' For a moment he sounded tired, as if he was weary of all this struggling.

Theresa leant back in the seat. In the black depths of her mind she felt a trace of fear. She glimpsed the surface of water, ruffled by the movement of long scaly bodies.

'No,' she whimpered. 'Please . . . No.'

'Yes,' Gideon said. 'It's the only way.'

Within Theresa there was a brief struggle. She fought against the thoughts which threatened to consume her. The long rows of teeth, the spray of blood.

Then Gideon looked down, his eyes averted, and her

fear hung suspended. She stared at him, and when he looked up again and into her face, she saw his eyes, so clear and dark and wide. It was as if there was a channel flowing from him into her. A channel of furious energy, which he released, which ate away her will, until there was nothing of her left. There was only Gideon inside her head, directing her thoughts, bringing up the long-hidden fears from the depths of her unconscious, drawing out the unbidden terror that was usually so deeply covered and embedded.

'You never understood.'

She could hear his voice. It was far off, a whispered echo.

'No one understands.'

He was trying to explain.

'If only you had helped me.'

It seemed as if he wanted someone to reach out a hand to him. Then his voice changed, as if he resented the evidence of his own weakness. The tone became sharp and shrill.

'But I don't need anyone. I never have. I'll be all right on my own.'

There was a catch in his voice. He was torn between independence and need.

'I wanted . . .' he began. 'But nobody liked me,' he continued. 'Nobody tried to understand. All they ever wanted to do was control me and tell me what to do.'

As he talked on, Theresa felt the fears floating in her head like an ominous mist. It broke open, so that she wanted to scream out, and then closed again, obscuring the haunting vision of blood and death.

Then Gideon stopped talking. He looked at her for a moment. His face was quite blank, and she felt her terror subside.

'Theresa,' he whispered. He was like a little boy lost. 'Theresa?' It was a question. He wanted to be given answers. He wanted to be looked after and cared for.

For one instant Theresa saw the absolute loneliness in which Gideon had always lived. Wanting, but not daring, to tell someone about himself, about the fearsome power that he had. A small child without friends. And like a child, striking out fretfully when he was hurt. Striking out – but with what dreadful consequences.

'Gideon.' Theresa's voice was soft. She wanted to befriend him, but it was all too late.

'No,' he said, and his manner changed yet again.

He looked at her with the hard eyes of a hawk. A bird of prey looking down at its victim.

'It's no use, Theresa. You'd never understand, not really.'

Gideon stood up and Theresa began to shake.

'It's time, Theresa,' he said. 'It's time to go.'

28

'Come along, Theresa,' he said.

She stood up, and stiffly and mechanically she walked along beside him.

'You know where we're going, don't you?'

It was more like a cruel taunt than a question.

'Of course you know,' Gideon said. 'Everyone knows the answer to that question. For each person the answer is different. But they all know.' He looked across at her. 'Your nightmare,' he said. 'The thing that you fear most. Everyone has a nightmare, don't they, a secret thing that they keep locked away. Sometimes it's hidden so deeply that they hardly know it's there themselves. That one particular thing that they fear the most.' He was gloating. 'You know where we're going, don't you, Theresa.'

The nightmare. The secret fear. She struggled to remember.

Gideon took the purse out of Theresa's handbag and passed the money over the counter, and then they both pushed through the turnstile.

The nightmare. Theresa dimly recalled her father sitting by the side of her bed and holding her. *You've had a bad dream, darling*, he was saying. Far-off days. A long time ago.

She was walking beside Gideon. Along the path. Past the elephant house. Past the bear pit. Gideon faltered. She felt him hesitate.

'It's funny,' Gideon said. 'Usually I can see everything so clearly. But with you there's something hidden, something at the edge of your fear that I cannot quite see.' He shrugged. 'But it doesn't really matter.'

They came to the reptile house and Gideon led her inside. A few people were standing about, looking at the snakes and lizards. Theresa felt an emanation from Gideon's mind thrusting out, and suddenly the heat in the room seemed intense and oppressive. The people inside started, felt hot and faint, and rushed out of the exit.

Gideon laughed. 'It's all so easy,' he said.

Now that the hall was empty he closed the doors and bolted them. He led the way past the glass-fronted vivaria where the snakes coiled on beds of sand or hung from the branches of simulated trees. At the far end of the hall, steps led up to a little gallery.

'We're there, Theresa,' Gideon said. 'We're there.'

They climbed the steps and stood on the balcony.

'Come on, Theresa. Look.'

Theresa walked forward. A low wall, and above it two metal rails. She put her hands on the top rail and looked down. Below her was a grey, muddy pool, surrounded by reeds. She looked closer; she couldn't see anything else. The air was hot, strangely hot. There was sweat on her face. She dabbed at her forehead with the end of her scarf. And all the time she was looking down into the distant pool.

Behind her, Gideon spoke. 'Jump,' he said. 'Jump.' His voice was insistent. 'Jump.'

'I won't do it,' she screamed out. She stared down at the water. It was unnaturally quiet. Then she saw two long black shapes moving steadily forward, cutting through the water. Crocodiles.

'Jump,' he said. 'It's what you want.'

She was leaning forward, looking down. For a moment the water was tempting. So cool. In that second she almost jumped. Then, into her mind, came the memory of the fire. She saw again the flames beating against the walls of the house, heard the cracking of the windows. And, worst of all, she saw her father's arm, reaching out.

She held on to the rail, clinging with tightened fingers. 'I mustn't let go,' she thought.

Something was pushing her forward, compelling her. She could feel Gideon inside her head whispering with the sound of her own voice.

'Let yourself go, Theresa. Down into the water. Down into the lovely cool water.'

'Don't make me,' she whimpered. 'I don't want to.' There was a terrible urge inside her to jump down into that seething pit of crocodiles and to end the agony that she felt. There was only one thing that held her back: the memory of the fire. He had killed them. She thought of the two pale faces in the flames and her anger burned hotly inside her.

She swung round to face him. 'You are evil,' she said. 'It was your fire. You were the cause.' And suddenly the flames were bright in her eyes. Her hatred flared up. 'I loathe you,' she said. 'And everything you've done. You deserve to die.'

He took a step backwards, shocked at the ferocity of

her anger. Their eyes locked together. It was a battle of wills.

Theresa could feel him probing for a weakness inside her head, but her hatred made her strong.

'You can't escape me, Theresa,' he said, but his voice sounded hollow.

She laughed. 'You'll burn,' she said. 'You'll burn and I'll be glad.'

Gideon winced, and she almost weakened. Her hands stretched out for the rail again. She could feel his mind bearing down upon her. She *must not* let go. Drawing her eyes away from his, she focused them on the blue and black patterns on her silk scarf. 'Remember the fire,' she whispered. 'It will burn you as it burnt them. You *won't* escape it.' She was gripping the rail so tightly her fingers were aching. She saw the taut white skin of her knuckles, the straining tendons, the red tapered nails. 'I won't let go,' she told him defiantly. 'But *you* will.' She closed her eyes. Below her was the murky water, but twisting within her were the fierce flames of the fire. Behind her she heard Gideon's scream. She drove his voice from her head and forced it back into his own. It was as if her hatred was reflecting back his power.

'I'm burning!' His voice was a wild and tortured scream.

When she glanced back at him she could see that he was tearing his hair with his hands. 'Please, Theresa.' He was whining, and pleading. But she knew that she must not weaken. It would be fatal. He would have no mercy. He would kill her as he had killed all the others.

'Please, God, let it be over,' she whispered. Her head was bursting with the pressure, the effort to keep him at bay. She turned back and leant against the rails. She could still feel the temptation inside her. The water would be cool. The conflict was so intense that everything became confused. She had no idea who she was fighting, or why.

She only knew that she must continue. Voices inside her head.

'Jump, Theresa. Hang on, Theresa.'

'The cool water. Don't make me.'

Then, suddenly, a voice from the past which she recognised. Her father's voice. He was sitting beside her. *What's the matter, Theresa? A bad dream?*

She stared at the water below her. Not a dream. But something was coming back to her. When she was a girl, a very small child, she had dreamt of *this*.

'Jump, Theresa, jump. It's what you want.'

Gideon's voice sounded desperate.

'*No*,' she screamed, and she knew now that she would never submit to him. She turned round to look at him, but he was already moving, running towards the rail. 'Oh my God,' she cried out, for she had seen all this before.

Over the rail he went and down into the water. And that part of the dream which had always been hidden from her because it was too terrible to see, she now witnessed in reality. It was the violent death of Gideon.

As his body touched the water the crocodiles fell upon him. Their tails threshing and churning up the water, they tore at his flesh with their enormous jaws. She saw the sharp teeth bite into his body and rip open the skin. Blood spurted up in a fine spray. She saw the grey lines of sinew strung out along the whitened bones. Then the teeth snapped shut again and the bones cracked. Remnants of flesh floated on the water and were at once consumed.

Theresa gasped in absolute horror. In a matter of minutes the body had disappeared down the maws of those savage animals. No trace remained, except the pink blush of blood on the surface of the rippling water. It was over. Theresa stood up. The air seemed cooler now.

She turned and went down the steps. There would be explanations to give. She would tell some sort of story of what had happened, but she would not tell the truth. No one would believe her. No one believed that dreams could become real, that the dark recesses of nightmares were linked inseparably with reality.

Theresa walked across the hall and threw open the doors. The sun slanted down across the buildings. She squinted in the bright light. She was quite numb, yet she felt a vast sense of relief. She had met with the secret fear of her childhood, conquered the old shadow which had fallen across her nights. The nightmare had happened, but now it was over. She was free of it at last.

FICTION

HORROR/OCCULT/NASTY		
☐ **Death Walkers**	Gary Brandner	£1.50
☐ **The Howling**	Gary Brandner	£1.50
☐ **Return of the Howling**	Gary Brandner	£1.50
☐ **The Sanctuary**	Glenn Chandler	£1.50
☐ **The Tribe**	Glenn Chandler	£1.10
☐ **The Black Castle**	Leslie Daniels	£1.25
☐ **The Big Goodnight**	Judy Gardiner	£1.25
☐ **Rattlers**	Joseph L. Gilmore	£1.25
☐ **The Nestling**	Charles L. Grant	£1.75
☐ **Slither**	John Halkin	£1.25
☐ **The Unholy**	John Halkin	£1.25
☐ **The Skull**	Shaun Hutson	£1.25
☐ **Pestilence**	Edward Jarvis	£1.50
☐ **The Beast Within**	Edward Levy	£1.25
☐ **Night Killers**	Richard Lewis	£1.25
☐ **Spiders**	Richard Lewis	£1.25
☐ **The Web**	Richard Lewis	£1.10
☐ **Bloodthirst**	Mark Ronson	£1.00
☐ **Ghoul**	Mark Ronson	95p
☐ **Ogre**	Mark Ronson	95p
☐ **Deathbell**	Guy N. Smith	£1.00
☐ **Doomflight**	Guy N. Smith	£1.10
☐ **The Lurkers**	Guy N. Smith	£1.25
☐ **Manitou Doll**	Guy N. Smith	£1.25
☐ **Satan's Snowdrop**	Guy N. Smith	£1.00
☐ **The Beast of Kane**	Cliff Twemlow	£1.50
☐ **The Pike**	Cliff Twemlow	£1.25
SCIENCE FICTION		
☐ **More Things in Heaven**	John Brunner	£1.50
☐ **The Proud Robot**	Henry Kuttner	£1.50
☐ **Death's Master**	Tanith Lee	£1.50
☐ **Electric Forest**	Tanith Lee	£1.25
☐ **The Dancers of Arun**	Elizabeth A. Lynn	£1.50
☐ **A Different Light**	Elizabeth A. Lynn	£1.50
☐ **The Northern Girl**	Elizabeth A. Lynn	£1.50
☐ **Balance of Power**	Brian M. Stableford	£1.75
WESTERNS – Blade Series – Matt Chisholm		
☐ **No. 5 The Colorado Virgins**		85p
☐ **No. 6 The Mexican Proposition**		85p
☐ **No. 8 The Nevada Mustang**		85p
☐ **No. 9 The Montana Deadlock**		85p
☐ **No. 10 The Cheyenne Trap**		95p
☐ **No. 11 The Navaho Trail**		95p
☐ **No. 12 The Last Act**		95p

FICTION

CRIME – WHODUNNIT

☐ **Thou Shell of Death**	Nicholas Blake	£1.25
☐ **The Widow's Cruise**	Nicholas Blake	£1.25
☐ **The Worm of Death**	Nicholas Blake	95p
☐ **The Long Divorce**	Edmund Crispin	£1.50
☐ **King and Joker**	Peter Dickinson	£1.25
☐ **The Last House-Party**	Peter Dickinson	£1.50
☐ **A Pride of Heroes**	Peter Dickinson	£1.50
☐ **The Seals**	Peter Dickinson	£1.50
☐ **Sleep and His Brother**	Peter Dickinson	£1.50
☐ **Firefly Gadroon**	Jonathan Gash	£1.50
☐ **The Vatican Rip**	Jonathan Gash	£1.50
☐ **Blood and Judgment**	Michael Gilbert	£1.10
☐ **Close Quarters**	Michael Gilbert	£1.10
☐ **Death of a Favourite Girl**	Michael Gilbert	£1.50
☐ **The Etruscan Net**	Michael Gilbert	£1.25
☐ **The Night of the Twelfth**	Michael Gilbert	£1.25
☐ **Silence Observed**	Michael Innes	£1.00
☐ **There Came Both Mist and Snow**	Michael Innes	95p
☐ **Go West, Inspector Ghote**	H.R.F. Keating	£1.50
☐ **Inspector Ghote Draws a Line**	H.R.F. Keating	£1.50
☐ **Inspector Ghote Plays a Joker**	H.R.F. Keating	£1.50
☐ **The Murder of the Maharajah**	H.R.F. Keating	£1.50
☐ **The Perfect Murder**	H.R.F. Keating	£1.50
☐ **The Dutch Shoe Mystery**	Ellery Queen	£1.60
☐ **The French Powder Mystery**	Ellery Queen	£1.25
☐ **The Siamese Twin Mystery**	Ellery Queen	95p
☐ **The Spanish Cape Mystery**	Ellery Queen	£1.10
☐ **Copper, Gold and Treasure**	David Williams	£1.75
☐ **Treasure by Degrees**	David Williams	£1.75
☐ **Unholy Writ**	David Williams	£1.60

NON-FICTION

WAR

☐ **The Battle of Malta**	Joseph Attard	£1.50
☐ **The Black Angels**	Rupert Butler	£1.50
☐ **Gestapo**	Rupert Butler	£1.50
☐ **Hand of Steel**	Rupert Butler	£1.35
☐ **Legions of Death**	Rupert Butler	£1.75
☐ **The Air Battle for Malta**	Lord James Douglas-Hamilton MP	£1.50
☐ **Auschwitz and the Allies**	Martin Gilbert	£4.95
☐ **Sigh for a Merlin**	Alex Henshaw	£1.50
☐ **Hitler's Secret Life**	Glen B. Infield	£1.50
☐ **Spitfire into Battle**	Group Captain Duncan Smith	£1.75
☐ **Women Beyond the Wire**	Lavinia Warner and John Sandilands	£1.95

FICTION

GENERAL		
☐ The Patriarch	Chaim Bermant	£1.75
☐ The Free Fishers	John Buchan	£1.50
☐ Midwinter	John Buchan	£1.50
☐ A Prince of the Captivity	John Buchan	£1.50
☐ The Eve of Saint Venus	Anthony Burgess	£1.10
☐ Nothing Like the Sun	Anthony Burgess	£1.50
☐ The Wanting Seed	Anthony Burgess	£1.50
☐ The Other Woman	Colette	£1.50
☐ Retreat From Love	Colette	£1.60
☐ Prizzi's Honour	Richard Condon	£1.75
☐ The Whisper of the Axe	Richard Condon	£1.75
☐ King Hereafter	Dorothy Dunnett	£2.95
☐ Pope Joan	Lawrence Durrell	£1.35
☐ The Country of her Dreams	Janice Elliott	£1.35
☐ Secret Places	Janice Elliott	£1.35
☐ Letter to a Child Never Born	Oriana Fallaci	£1.00
☐ A Man	Oriana Fallaci	£1.95
☐ Rich Little Poor Girl	Terence Feely	£1.75
☐ Marital Rites	Margaret Forster	£1.50
☐ Grimalkin's Tales	Gardiner, Ronson, Whitelaw	£1.60
☐ Who Was Sylvia?	Judy Gardiner	£1.50
☐ Lost and Found	Julian Gloag	£1.95
☐ La Presidenta	Lois Gould	£1.75
☐ A Sea-Change	Lois Gould	£1.50
☐ Black Summer	Julian Hale	£1.75
☐ Duncton Wood	William Horwood	£2.50
☐ The Stonor Eagles	William Horwood	£2.95
☐ The Man Who Lived at the Ritz	A.E. Hotchner	£1.65
☐ The Fame Game	Rona Jaffe	£1.50

NAME ....

ADDRESS ....

....

Write to Hamlyn Paperbacks Cash Sales, PO Box 11, Falmouth, Cornwall TR10 9EN

Please indicate order and enclose remittance to the value of the cover price plus:

U.K.: Please allow 45p for the first book plus 20p for the second book and 14p for eac additional book ordered, to a maximum charge of £1.63.

B.F.P.O. & EIRE: Please allow 45p for the first book plus 20p for the second book an 14p per copy for the next 7 books, thereafter 8p per book.

OVERSEAS: Please allow 75p for the first book and 21p per copy for each addition book.

Whilst every effort is made to keep prices low it is sometimes necessary to increase cov prices and also postage and packing rates at short notice. Hamlyn Paperbacks reserve th right to show new retail prices on covers which may differ from those previously adve tised in the text or elsewhere.